WINTER AT THE STABLES ON MUDDYPUDDLE LANE

Heart-warming, uplifting romance

Etti Summers

CHAPTER ONE

'You're giving this to me **now**?' Megan Barnes stared at the card and the words written on it, and shook her head. She was trying to hold back tears and so far she was succeeding, but she didn't think she'd manage it for much longer.

Richard winced. 'It was what Jeremy wanted and I've never deviated from his instructions; you know that.'

'But it's December – far too cold to go horse riding.'

'Look,' her brother-in-law said. 'I didn't have anything to do with this. Or any of the other—' he cleared his throat '—gifts.'

'I used to ride when I was a girl,' she said, sitting down abruptly. They were in her living room, the place where Richard usually handed her the envelopes Jeremy had left for her since he'd died. And every time Richard did so, it was as though her heart was being torn from her chest and she was losing Jeremy all over again.

Richard, who was Jeremy's brother and the executor of his will, said, 'If it's any consolation, this is the final one. There are no more.'

'Thank goodness for that. I don't think I can take any more.' The last one had instructed her to go diving. She and Jeremy had intended doing it when they went on holiday to Turkey, but the holiday had to be cancelled. In the end, Megan had dived without him, off the coast of West Wales. It had been a far chillier experience than the one they'd planned. But during those brief minutes on the seabed, she'd felt closer to her husband than ever. Megan gulped, wishing he had been with her; he would have loved it. But this last and final gift wasn't **their** dream. This one belonged to her and her alone.

'How do you feel about it?' Richard dropped into the chair opposite and nodded at the card she was holding in her hand.

'Horse riding in the snow?' she mused. 'I did that once, when I was fourteen. It was magical.'

It was so sweet of Jeremy to have remembered. She recalled what they'd been doing when she'd shared the memory with her husband. Except, he hadn't been her husband then. He'd been a man she'd fancied rotten and it was their third date. He'd taken her to a repurposed lighthouse somewhere in North Devon for a meal. It must have cost him a fortune because there had only been five tables in the room at the top where the light would once have shone, and it was rather exclusive. She'd known then that she wanted to marry him.

She'd got her wish.

Her only regret was that he'd died so young. Forty-three was no age. He hadn't reached his prime yet. But cancer had snatched him from her with grim and deadly determination.

Megan let out a shaky sigh. 'Hit me with it,' she instructed.

The card told her the bare minimum. Jeremy had undoubtedly left more details with Richard, which her brother-in-law always followed to the letter.

'Five lessons, and the last one is to be a hack – I think that's the word – in the hills when it snows.'

'This one can't have been easy for you to arrange,' she said, and when he gave her a puzzled frown she added, 'Arranging for it to snow on the very day I am to go riding.'

'Very funny,' he said, shaking his head at her. He hesitated. 'It's nice to see you crack a joke again.'

Is that what she'd done? It had been so long since she'd found anything remotely funny, she'd assumed her humour had gone for good, that it had died along with the love of her life.

'Don't read too much into it,' she warned. 'I probably won't do it again.'

'It's been nineteen months.'

'So? Does grief have an expiry date?'

'Of course not, and I feel his loss as keenly as you, but you can't mourn him forever.'

'Who says I can't?'

'Jeremy.' Richard reached into his jacket pocket and put another envelope on the coffee table.

'What does it say?' Megan was scared to read it. She could guess what was in it, and she wasn't ready. She didn't think she ever would be.

'Read it,' Richard said, getting to his feet. He gave her shoulder a squeeze. 'Life is for living. Jeremy knew that – he wants you to know it, too.'

Wants...not **wanted**. That was the problem with her husband speaking to her from beyond the grave – both she and Richard had a tendency to refer to him as though he were still alive.

'Take care of yourself,' her brother-in-law said as he always did on parting. To be fair to him, he tried his utmost to make sure she was okay, but he had a wife and children, and a demanding job. He had enough on his plate without her and her steadfast and inconsolable grief.

'I'll try,' she replied, as she always did.

Taking care of herself was a hit-and-miss affair, with eating regularly being the major issue. When she looked in the mirror, she didn't recognise the skeletal pale wraith staring back at her. At least the horse wouldn't have a sturdy burden to carry. She had lost nearly a third of her body weight since Jeremy died, but she consoled herself with the knowledge that she'd had a fair bit of padding to spare, so it looked more dramatic than it was.

Richard, however, was convinced she was fading away.

She wished the letter sitting on the table in front of her would do exactly that. She wished Richard hadn't given it to her. She wished Jeremy hadn't felt the need to write it. But he'd known her better than she knew herself – he'd anticipated her desolation, and the gifts had been his way of helping her cope.

This last dream wasn't his, though. It had been hers, and the symbolism of doing something purely for herself, something he'd had no interest in, wasn't lost on her.

Taking a deep breath and with tears trickling unnoticed down her face, Megan reached for the letter.

Nathan never knew how to behave around crying women. Was he supposed to give them a hug? Pretend it wasn't happening? Make them a cup of tea?

In the end he settled for muttering a trite, 'There, there,' and patting Charity Jones on the arm, whilst wishing he was anywhere but here.

The stables on Muddypuddle Lane and the surrounding countryside was usually his favourite place to be. Except for today.

'Why don't you see if Timothy will buy him?' Nathan suggested.

'He'd love to, but he's not got the time to look after him, and Midnight needs to be ridden more often than Timothy can manage. You know how the horse gets when he isn't ridden enough.'

Nathan sighed. He did know. Midnight could be a right pain in the rear end. 'Do you want me to deal with this fella?'

'Do you mind?'

Nathan minded a lot, but he minded Charity's tears more. He shrugged. 'I suppose not.'

He completely understood her distress, even though Midnight wasn't her horse. Midnight belonged to her twin sister, Faith, and the two girls had stabled their animals here for years. But Faith was moving to Norwich to live and she couldn't take the beast with her. And neither could she afford to continue to keep it at the stables because the horse had lived here free of charge in exchange for Faith's labour. Charity had the same arrangement with her mare, Storm.

And that was where Charity's tears stemmed from – Faith was selling Midnight, and nothing would be the same again. Nathan got that, he really did. But he still felt uncomfortable being around Charity while she was so upset, and neither did he particularly want to get involved in the sale of the horse. But what else could he do? She was in no fit state to deal with the man who was coming to look at the animal, and besides which, she was rather on the young side, being only twenty-five (he was allowed to call her young because he was forty-seven) and he didn't want anyone to take advantage of her.

Charity said, 'Faith had asked Mum to deal with it, but Mum's got enough to do with Grandma. She's going to have to see about her going into Honeymead soon.'

'At least it's local,' Nathan said. 'And your grandma will see you almost every day.' Charity worked in the care home in Picklewick, so she'd be able to keep an eye on her grandmother. 'Why can't Faith see this fella herself?' He didn't think it right she'd asked others to do what she should be doing herself.

'She can't face it,' Charity said.

Nathan almost replied, **and you can?** but he held his tongue; there was no point in him rubbing in the fact that she couldn't face it, either.

She thanked him profusely and he watched her walk across the yard. Both Charity and Faith were lovely young ladies, but Charity was probably his favourite of the two. She was quieter and more introverted than her twin, and if he'd been lucky enough to have had kids he would have loved to have had a daughter just like her.

It was his one big regret in life that he and Lynnette had never had children. The time had never seemed to be right, and suddenly it was very wrong indeed and they had ended up getting a divorce. She'd gone on to have two children with her new partner, whilst Nathan hadn't even entertained the idea of having a relationship with anyone else.

It was too late now, of course. Even if he managed to find someone who'd be willing to put up with him, he didn't fancy having kids at his age. He was too set in his ways for nappies and sleepless nights.

He was happy as he was, with only himself to answer to. And his boss Petra, of course. She owned the stables along with her uncle, Amos, and she ran a tight ship. But that's the way he liked it. A person knew what was what with Petra; she didn't pussyfoot around – she told it like it was. And as long as he did his job, she let him get on with it.

The arrangement suited them both; she trusted him to know what he was doing, and he was happy not to have anyone breathing down his neck.

Ah, this must be the fella, Nathan thought, as he saw a car trundling up the lane, bouncing over the potholes. Come the spring he'd have to fill those in; some of them would put a moon crater to shame, they were that deep. However, winter wasn't the best month to try laying tarmac.

'Luca, is it?' Nathan asked as the car drew to a halt and a man got out. 'Here about buying a horse?'

'That's me.'

Nathan gave him a quick up-and-down glance. Mid-thirties by the look of him, slim, athletic, not bad looking. Those white jodhpurs were a bit over-the-top, and his helmet looked brand new, but all Nathan hoped was that he knew his way around a horse. Midnight could be a bit of a handful, and wasn't suitable for an inexperienced rider.

Oh, well, best get this over with.

'He's happy to give the full asking price,' Nathan said to Petra after Luca had left. 'So you'd better let Faith know she's sold her horse.'

'When will he come for him?' Petra was sitting on a small stool in the barn, busily milking Princess. It was a scene reminiscent of a bygone era, a rural pastoral idyll, with the goat contentedly munching on some vegetable peelings, and Petra with her breath misting above her head as she milked the animal by hand. All that was needed to complete the scene was for her to be wearing a long dress and a pinafore, and maybe a frilly cotton cap on her head.

Nathan scratched his chin. 'Ah, now, that's the thing. He wants to know if he can leave him here. He'll pay livery fees.'

'He better had. I'm not feeding that brute for nothing.'

Nathan knew she didn't mean it. Petra loved all the animals at the stables, and she might curse them herself, but woe betide anyone else who did.

'I've left his number in the office,' Nathan said. 'He'll be wanting a vet to check him over before he signs on the dotted line.'

'Fair enough. Does he want to bring his own vet in, or will he be okay with using the practice in Picklewick?'

'No idea,' Nathan replied, chirpily. He'd done his bit, the rest was up to Faith, Petra and Luca to sort out.

'Can he handle him?' Petra asked.

'I think so.' This new fella didn't have too bad a seat on him, Nathan had thought as he'd watched him put the horse through its paces. He'd seemed confident enough and he hadn't put up with any nonsense from Midnight. He'd even got the animal over a few jumps, and not a bad height at that. The man had clearly done some jumping in the past.

Nathan was about to get back to work when the phone rang, echoing through the barn, sounding shrill and tinny over the loudspeaker.

Petra glanced up. 'Do you mind getting that? Amos has gone to the supermarket and if I leave Princess half milked, she won't be happy.'

Princess, when she was unhappy, was a right madam, so Nathan nodded and trudged over to the office, glad of a chance to be in the warm for a few minutes. Winter had its own special beauty, but that didn't mean to say he was a fan of the cold.

'Muddypuddle Stables,' he said gruffly, picking up the handset.

The person on the other end was a woman. 'Hello, I, um, I've been gifted some riding lessons with your stables, five to be exact. Well, four, the fifth is meant to be a ride in the snow.'

'In the snow,' Nathan repeated woodenly. 'Is that right?' He didn't know Petra was doing snow rides, or sunshine rides, or any weather rides. As far as he knew, you booked a ride and you took pot luck when it came to the elements. The most common weather was overcast, or rain. You didn't get to choose.

'Yes,' the woman continued. 'Was it arranged via yourself?'

'Nope. With Petra, I expect. Or Amos.'

'Oh, I see. Could you check for me, please?'

'Wait there.' Nathan put the handset on the desk and went back to the barn. 'There's a woman on the phone saying you can make it snow,' he said, chuckling to himself.

'Pardon?' Petra stopped milking and she straightened up. Princess, cross at the cessation of service, bleated loudly and pawed at the pile of hay she'd been working her way through.

'A woman on the phone has been given four lessons and a ride in the snow,' Nathan said, pulling a face. 'I think that's what she said.'

Petra frowned for a moment, then her forehead cleared. 'Ah, I remember. Her husband – he's dead now, by the way – arranged for her to have a few lessons to refresh her riding skills, then a hack on a day when the snow is down.'

'I see.'

'Don't give me that look,' Petra said. 'I can't guarantee it'll snow this winter, but it usually does. Book her in for me, would you? Thanks.'

Nathan stomped back across the yard and returned to the office to resume the call. 'Amos is out and Petra is busy,' he said, 'but she's told me what's what, so I'll book you in for your first lesson.'

'I don't need a lesson, as such. I can ride, although it's been a good few years since I was on the back of a horse.'

'You said you'd been given four lessons?'

'That's right. And a hack.'

'Then that's what you'll have. What day were you thinking of?'

'Oh, um...Friday?'

Nathan grabbed the diary and a pen, and flipped to the correct page.

'What time? I'm assuming this lesson is a private one?'

'It is,' the woman confirmed. 'I'm free all day, so whatever suits you.'

'Two o'clock?'

'That's fine. Um, I take it you have a helmet I can borrow? I've not ridden for quite a few years.'

'So you said. It's a good job you'll be having some lessons,' Nathan retorted. 'Yes, we've got hats. What's the name?'

'Megan Barnes.'

'Right, we'll see you on Friday at two,' he said, snapping the diary shut.

'Yes, Friday. Two pm. I'll be there.'

After he'd come off the phone, he thought she'd sounded nervous, and he recalled what Petra had said...something about a dead husband buying her lessons. He couldn't have died all that long ago, Nathan surmised, then felt a little guilty for being so short with her.

Oh, well, he said to himself, it wasn't as though he'd have to speak to her again. Petra would be taking the lesson, whilst he got on with whatever jobs needed doing.

He didn't like being around crying women, and he liked being around grieving ones even less.

CHAPTER TWO

The weather forecast said there might be a white Christmas this year, but Megan wasn't holding her breath. They were barely into December, and she didn't have faith that anyone was able to accurately predict more than a day or so ahead. Sometimes they couldn't even manage to get today's weather right she grumbled to herself, when it began to drizzle as she pulled into the lane leading to the stables. It was supposed to have been fine all day, if overcast, but at least the riding lesson was indoors. Long gone were the days when she'd happily go out in all weathers. When she was a girl, the only thing she'd cared about was being on the back of a horse, and in those days she'd been too full of youthful enthusiasm and zest for life to feel the cold. But neither had she had to sort out sodden clothes and muddy boots, because her mum had done that for her.

Thinking about her mother made Megan recall her latest visit, and her mum's reaction when she informed her of Jeremy's final gift. Her mother had sniffed and pulled a face, more intent on showing her disapproval of a woman of Megan's age risking climbing onto the back of a horse, than appreciating the romantic and incredibly sad gesture.

Her mother's condemnation had only served to push Megan into making the decision to phone the stables and book herself in for her first lesson.

She knew it was childish, but it typified their relationship.

Now though, Megan was beginning to regret the whole thing, beginning with the terse manner of the man on the other end of the phone when she rang the stables to book the lesson, and ending with her conviction that her mum was probably right, and she was probably too old to go riding. Jeremy, bless him, still used to think of her as the young woman he'd married. He'd never seemed to notice her ever-growing number of grey hairs, or the deepening lines around her eyes. If he could see her now though, she thought he might be shocked. She'd aged about ten years since he'd passed away, and when she looked in the mirror Megan didn't recognise herself. She was forty-two but looked a decade older. His death had taken its toll on her, emotionally, mentally and physically.

It was only to be expected. It was impossible to lose the only man she would ever love and come through it unscathed. To her credit, she looked better now than she had in the months immediately after he'd died, when her skin had been pallid and grey and she'd moved like an invalid, slowly and carefully. The blow it had dealt to her soul had been reflected in her body, and she'd almost welcomed it as a physical sign of the absolute grief she'd felt.

The grief hadn't gone away and she suspected it never would, but she was learning to live with it, absorbing it into herself, allowing it to become part of who she was rather than having it draped over her like a heavy cloak, weighing her down.

Sighing deeply, she switched the windscreen wipers off and sat in the car for a moment, relishing the warmth, because she had a feeling it was going to be bitterly cold outside.

And she was right, she discovered as she clambered out, ungainly in her haste to retrieve her old coat from the back seat and grab her brand-new riding boots. She'd debated the wisdom of buying them, but unlike the helmet which she intended to borrow, wearing someone else's riding boots wasn't an option she fancied, and she didn't have anything suitable that she was prepared to ruin; mud and horse poop wasn't going to do her usual footwear much good.

After slipping her trainers off and changing into her boots, she was as ready as she ever would be. Spotting a sign that said Reception, she headed towards it and hoped she wouldn't bump into the man she'd spoken to on the phone. When she'd questioned Richard, he'd informed her that when he'd helped Jeremy set up the lessons, it had been through a woman. But that was nearly two years ago, and staff might have changed. Megan had been surprised anyone had remembered and was going to honour the pre-paid lessons.

'Hello?' she called, entering the side of the large metal structure and finding herself in a corridor with an office to the

right, a toilet to the left and a viewing
gallery set out with hard plastic chairs
directly in front of her. Beyond it, she
could see an arena and guessed that was
where her lesson would take place.

'You must be my two o'clock,' a female
voice behind her said, and Megan jumped
in alarm.

'Goodness, I didn't hear you,' she said,
clutching a hand to her throat. 'Yes, I'm
she.'

'I've put you on an old lady called Mabel,'
the woman told her, 'just to see how you
get on. If I think you can cope with a less
steady horse, I'll put you up on a different
one next time.'

'Oh, right, um...I have ridden before. Quite
a bit, actually.'

'When was that? My name is Petra, by the way. Petra Kelly. I run the place.'

'Nice to meet you, Petra.' Megan held out a hand and Petra's eyebrows twitched. She shook it though. 'Um, when I was a teenager,' Megan admitted.

'That's got to be a couple of decades ago.'

'And the rest.' Megan smiled, appreciating the woman's tact.

'Horse riding is a bit like riding a bike,' Petra said. 'You don't totally forget but it does take your body a while to get used to it again, and regain your confidence. But horses aren't bikes and they can sense when you're nervous. Mabel won't bat an eyelid – she's as steady as a rock.' Petra looked her straight in the eye. 'I was beginning to think you weren't coming. But I remember the man I spoke to telling me it might be a year or so, two even...My condolences,' she added.

Megan inclined her head, grateful the woman didn't do the sympathetic head-tilt that so many people did when faced with the recently bereaved. Except, it wasn't so recent any more – two years sounded an awful lot longer than twenty months.

Petra cleared her throat. 'Shall we get on? You told Nathan you needed a hat?'

'That's right.'

'Come through and you can try some on.'

Megan followed Petra into the office and saw the shelves of helmets stacked along one wall, and as she tried a couple on she filed Nathan's name away for future reference if she had the misfortune to speak to him again.

'How many horses do you have here?' she asked when, hat-fitting done, Petra showed her into the arena and the gentle old mare waiting for her.

'Three for customers to use, plus another three, one of which is mine and the other two which belong to the girls who work here. Then there are seventeen ponies, a donkey and a goat. No one rides the donkey. Or the goat, for that matter.'

Megan laughed. She had a vision of a small child perched on top of a goat. 'How long have you been here?' She stroked the animal's nose and the mare gazed back at her with doe-soft eyes. Megan had forgotten how lovely and whiskery a horse's nose could be, and she smiled as the fine hairs tickled her palm.

'All my life, on and off. My aunt and uncle owned the place and I used to visit every chance I could. Then Aunt Mags passed away and Amos needed the help, so I moved in when I was eighteen. Been here ever since. Wouldn't want to be anywhere else.' This last was said with a hint of belligerence, as though she'd been questioned about it in the past.

'If you find what you like doing, you should stick with it,' Megan said. 'I envy you – I still don't know what I want to do when I grow up.'

'What do you do, if you don't mind me asking? Here, let me sort the stirrups out and I'll give you a bunk up.'

Megan stood to the side to let Petra lengthen the stirrups. 'I work in HR.'

'From the tone of your voice you don't sound as though you like it,' Petra observed astutely.

'I don't,' Megan replied. Then her eyes widened. She'd not said that out loud before, but the thought had been lingering in the back of her mind for a while, without her being totally aware of it. Gosh...

Petra pulled a face. 'So don't do it. Here you go – stick your foot in there and I'll shove your backside.'

Megan did as she was told and found herself sitting astride the horse in one smooth movement.

'Gather the reins and ask her to walk on. A circle around the arena, should do it. You've paid for five sessions in all – if you're as competent as I hope you are, the final ride will be in the snow. The one before that can be a hack out onto the hills so you can get a feel for being outside on the horse. This one is to gauge where you are, so the other two will depend on what happens today. Is that okay with you?'

Megan nodded; she had a feeling Petra wasn't asking for her opinion or her input. She was simply telling her what was going to happen. The woman was almost as gruff as Nathan. Maybe it was a horsey thing.

As Megan and Mabel made their way to the far end of the arena and back again,

Megan asked, 'Is Nathan your husband or partner?'

'I'm not married, and he's not my partner in any sense of the word. He's a good bloke, though. I couldn't run the stables without him. Try trotting; I expect to see air between you and the saddle,' Petra warned.

Ouch, Megan had forgotten how hard on the thighs a rising trot was. Her leg muscles were screaming at her before she'd done a single lap, and she made a promise to herself that she'd do some squats at home before her next ride.

All too soon though, her hour was up and despite aching more than she'd ever ached in the past, she realised she'd had a fab time. Being on horseback had dredged up so many childhood memories, and she recalled how happy riding used to make her.

As she slid rather inelegantly from the saddle, she sent a silent thank you to her husband. She'd enjoyed herself immensely and couldn't wait for next week.

'Before I go, do you mind if I have a look around?' she asked.

'Be my guest. Just be careful about putting your fingers too near Princess's mouth, else she'll try to eat them. Princess is the goat.'

Megan took her hat off and shook out her hair. 'Shall I pop this back in the office?' She held up the hat.

'That'll be a help, thanks. When do you want your next lesson?' Petra was shortening the stirrups and sorting out the reins.

'Same time next week?'

Petra wrinkled her nose as she thought. 'When you go into the office check the diary on the desk. If two o'clock is free, write your name down.'

Megan blinked. That was very trusting. She wasn't sure she'd want anyone messing with her diary. Oh, well, if it worked for Petra who was she to criticise she thought, as she left Petra to see to the horse.

'Oh, hello.' Megan hesitated in the office doorway. She'd been about to enter when she'd spotted a man standing at the opposite end to the shelves of hats.

He had his back to her and was staring at a whiteboard filled with scribbled writing.

He put a tick next to one of the items, nodded to himself, then turned around. 'Hello, who are you?'

'Megan Barnes. I was just putting this back.' She held up her helmet and as she did so, she could have sworn she heard the man mutter, 'Bugger.'

It took her a moment to guess why that was and when she did, she tried not to smile. If she wasn't sorely mistaken, the man was none other than Nathan, who she'd spoken to on the phone. And he looked rather dismayed to see her.

Good.

The last person Nathan wanted to see was Megan Barnes. He knew she was booked in for a lesson today because he'd booked her in himself, but he'd thought he was safe enough in the office. Clearly, he was wrong.

'Petra told me to put myself down for another lesson next week,' Megan said, hesitating before adding, 'If that's okay?' She glanced at the diary on the desk, then turned around to put her helmet back on the shelf.

When she turned back to him and he got
a proper look at her, he was surprised at
how attractive she was. He guessed her
to be a few years younger than him, but it
was difficult to tell. He'd never been very
good at women's ages. This one could be
anywhere between thirty and forty.

She had longish hair, falling past her
shoulders, in a glossy brown with the odd
grey hair showing at her temples. It
seemed she didn't colour it, and he quite
liked that. He much preferred the natural
look, and she didn't appear to be wearing
any makeup either, so that was a plus as
far as he was concerned. Her cheekbones
were quite prominent, and she had a
generous mouth which was made for
smiling, but from the haunted expression
in her eyes he didn't think she did much
of that.

She stared right back at him, her gaze
steady and direct.

Nathan coughed and bent his head towards the diary. The book was dog-eared and well used. 'What day?' he asked.

'Same day, same time, please.'

He used a slightly grubby finger to flick to the correct week then he ran it down the page until he came to the right day. 'I'll write you in,' he said, picking up a pen and scrawling her name across the page with 2 p.m. next to it. 'There – all done.'

'Thank you.' She paused, and for a moment he thought she was going to say something, but she didn't. All she did was smile politely and walk to the door.

He waited for her to leave and watched her walk into the yard. Expecting her to drive off, to his consternation he saw her heading in the opposite direction from the car park and he hastened after her, wondering what she was up to.

She glanced over her shoulder as she heard his footsteps and came to a halt, looking nervous. 'Petra said it was okay if I had a look around,' she said. She gave him a small smile that didn't reach her eyes. 'I've already been warned about Princess.'

Nathan saw her gaze travel around the yard. He had already brought some of the animals in from the fields because it was starting to get dark. None of the horses or ponies were left out overnight in the winter, so there were several equine heads peering over the half-doors, their ears pricked, waiting for their supper.

'He's a handsome fellow,' Megan said, as her gaze swept around the loose boxes and came to rest on Midnight, the horse that had just had a new owner.

In fact, there was the chap now, Nathan saw, as another car pulled into the car park.

Luca got out and gave him a nod. 'Everything all right?' he asked as he came closer.

'Couldn't be better,' Nathan said. 'I've brought him in for the night.' He jerked his head towards Midnight. 'He's got a fresh hay net, but I haven't given him any grain yet.'

'That's okay, I can do that.' Luca sauntered across the yard, heading straight for his horse. Megan's eyes followed him, then she caught Nathan watching her and she dropped her gaze.

Nathan wondered if she was in the market for a new husband. Luca was good-looking, and despite the outward confidence and slightly brash air, the brief contact Nathan had had with him revealed him to be a pleasant enough chap. He didn't mind getting his hands dirty, and he mucked out his horse's stall willingly enough even though the fee he paid Petra for continuing to house his animal at the stables included everything except for shoeing.

Anyway, it was none of Nathan's business who Megan looked at. As long as she didn't bother him, he didn't care what she did. 'I'd better get on,' he said. 'I've got the rest of the ponies to bring in.'

Luca said, 'I'd give you a hand but I can't stay long. I just thought I'd pop in for half an hour so we could get acquainted.' He patted Midnight's neck and the horse tossed his head.

Nathan grunted. He would have appreciated the help. An extra pair of hands around the place would come in handy. Faith and Charity used to do this between them, but now that Faith had sold Midnight, she was no longer obliged to help out at the stables. It was therefore down to him to bring the horses in if Petra was busy and if Charity was at work. He wondered if Petra was planning on hiring someone to replace Faith. He certainly hoped so, because his workload had increased quite a bit. Petra had even asked if he'd be willing to take a hack out if needed, but so far he hadn't had to, thank goodness.

'I can help, if you like?' Megan said, and Nathan was taken aback.

'Er, thank you, but I can manage.'

'It's no trouble,' she said, seeming rather insistent. 'I don't have anything to rush home for.' Stopping abruptly, she bit her lip.

Nathan winced; he hoped she wasn't going to mention her recent loss. He was sympathetic to her situation, but that didn't mean to say he wanted to be drawn into a discussion about it. Or worse – what if she began to cry? He shuddered, then felt guilty and prayed she hadn't noticed.

'How many of them are left to bring in?' she asked. 'Gosh, I haven't done anything like this since I was a girl.'

She suddenly looked more animated, and he didn't have the heart to repeat that he could manage on his own. What harm would it do? He usually brought the horses and ponies in two at a time, but with this woman to help he'd be able to bring in the last four without making two trips to the field.

'Go on, then,' he said. 'But if you get your foot trodden on, I'm not taking responsibility.'

Megan blinked at him. 'No doubt the stable has insurance,' she said.

'It does, but as I was saying, you offered to help, so if something happens it's on your own head.'

'Noted.'

'And you're going to get those mucky.' Nathan stared at her boots.

Megan looked down at them. 'That's what they're there for.'

They looked very new and rather shiny to him, but if she wanted to muck them up it was up to her. 'I'll fetch the lead ropes,' he said, and stamped off to the tack room, feeling rather out of sorts.

Nathan was mostly a taciturn man. He'd freely admit it. But rarely was he such a grouch, and he wondered why he was being so curmudgeonly now. For some reason Megan Barnes was bringing out the worst in him, and he couldn't understand why. He'd only spoken to her once on the phone, and he'd just met her in person today. His acquaintance of her added up to all of five minutes. But there was something about her that made him uneasy, and he couldn't put his finger on what. Was it because she was recently bereaved? Was he worried she might collapse into hysterics?

Possibly – Nathan halted in the act of lifting a couple of lead ropes off the hook, as he suddenly realised what was wrong. He was attracted to her.

The newfound knowledge didn't help his mood one little bit. He didn't want a woman in his life and he had no need of one; he was perfectly fine the way he was without the added complication of romance and relationships. He had his job, his friends and his little Jack Russell to keep him company and to keep him busy. And on the odd occasion he felt lonely, he'd give himself a good telling off and take the dog for a long walk.

Nathan snatched the lead ropes off their hooks in a fit of angst and clumped back to where he'd left her. But Megan was no longer there, and for a second he felt quite put out as he wondered whether she'd changed her mind and had gone home.

To his immense annoyance, his heart lifted when he spotted her in Midnight's loose box holding the animal's head whilst Luca checked his hooves, before his heart plunged to his boots as he realised a woman like her wouldn't look twice at a man like him. Luca was more her type.

He whirled on his heel, heading for the lane, eager to put a bit of distance between her and his wayward feelings, when he heard her call, 'Wait up,' and there was the sound of her footsteps hurrying behind him.

'Here,' he said, thrusting two of the lead ropes at her when she caught up. Megan took them without a murmur, but the look she gave him was enough. She clearly wasn't impressed with him. Nathan wasn't impressed with himself either, for that matter.

He knew he was behaving badly, so in an effort to appear less sullen, he asked, 'How was your riding lesson?' then shot her a quick look out of the corner of his eye.

She raised her eyebrows at his sudden friendliness but she answered readily enough. 'It was good, thanks. Petra was very patient with me. And so was Mabel.'

'Aye, she's a good 'un,' he said.

'Petra or the horse?'

It was Nathan's turn to raise his eyebrows, and to his surprise he chuckled. 'Both,' he said, and he saw her smile. 'Mabel is as calm and steady as they come, Petra not so much. But she's a damn fine horseman, and she's a good teacher, too.'

'Petra was right, riding isn't like riding a bike. You do lose some of your confidence. Mabel looked after me though.'

'She's good like that. Getting a bit long in the tooth now though, so she doesn't get ridden much these days. She'll be put out to pasture before long.'

'I expect you and Petra will miss her.'

Nathan shook his head. 'She's not going anywhere. She'll live out her days at the stables. Petra keeps all her animals, no matter how old or sick they get. Once an animal arrives at the stables it stays here until it's carried out in a box. Me included. Oh dear...'

Nathan wished he hadn't said that. He pulled a face and prepared to apologise, but when he risked glancing at her he saw that Megan's expression was calm and she didn't seem to have taken offence from his careless and unthinking remark.

'You're not that old, surely?' she asked him.

'Coming up for fifty,' he said. 'Although I suppose that's not old these days. In my grandad's day, you retired at sixty-five and you thought you were past it. You had maybe another five or ten years before you kicked the bucket.'

Dear god, he'd done it again. What was wrong with him? He didn't seem able to stop sticking his foot in his mouth.

'It's okay,' Megan said, seeing his embarrassment.

And he **was** embarrassed, very embarrassed. See, he said to himself, this was why he didn't like talking to people. Because he tended to put his foot in it and make an idiot of himself.

'It's funny how our language is littered with references to death,' Megan said, and Nathan drew in a deep breath.

Here we go, he thought. Thank god the gate to the field was only a few yards away and he could use the excuse of catching the ponies not to have to listen to her.

'You can't get away from it,' she was saying, 'so please don't restrict what you say because of me. I won't get upset and I won't take offence. Only yesterday I said to someone at work that I should have put on a thicker jumper because I was going to catch my death.'

Nathan felt a little better. 'Did you really?'

'No, I didn't.' She smiled at him. 'But I could very well have done, so please don't feel awkward. I'd hate for anyone to feel uncomfortable when they were talking to me.'

'It can't be easy,' Nathan said not wanting to get into a discussion, but feeling he had to say something. 'How long has it been?'

'Since my husband died? It's okay, you can say those words. Twenty months.'

Nathan jerked to a halt, one hand on the bolt, the other on the top bar ready to pull the gate open. 'Oh, I thought it was more recent.'

'Some days it feels very recent,' she said. 'Other days it feels like a lifetime. Jeremy, my husband, in cahoots with his brother, booked these riding lessons for me before he died. He arranged for me to do a few other things too, and Richard, that's my brother-in-law, has been doling them out to me on a regular basis. Riding in the snow is the last one.'

'That's um...' Nathan was lost for words. He wasn't sure whether it was a lovely thing to do, or an awful thing. It certainly kept her husband's memory alive for her, but on the other hand it also might stop

her from moving on. Heck, what did he
know? He'd never lost anyone; both his
parents were still alive and so were his
two siblings.

'Bizarre?' she said, completing his
sentence for him. 'Some people have said
so, and others have said how lucky I am.
To be honest, the jury is still out on that
one. Some days it's a tremendous comfort
to know he was thinking of my future
without him. Other days it's unbearable,
because I feel like he's still here when I
know he isn't.'

Yep, that was more or less what Nathan
had been thinking. Wisely he didn't say
that. Instead, he said, 'That one there and
that one are the easiest to catch,'
pointing to two of the ponies. 'The
chestnut is Tango, the cream one is
Parsnip. If you call them, they'll probably
come to you.'

He left her to it, whilst he carried on
trying to catch the terrible twosome – a

pair of Shetland ponies who refused to go anywhere without the other. They weren't keen on being brought in for the night either, and Nathan sometimes wondered what they got up to when they were left outside during the warmer months.

Eventually he caught one of them and, knowing the other would follow, he made his way back to the gate where Megan was waiting for him with her charges.

'Everything okay?' he asked.

'They were as good as gold.'

'That's because they're greedy, and they know they're going to get a bucket of warm mash.' He frowned, thinking she might think he was referring to mashed potato. 'Mash is a mix of grains and warm water, and other stuff like carrots, beets and apples.'

'I remember,' she said. 'The stables where I used to ride when I was younger fed their ponies the same sort of thing.'

'There you are!' Nathan exclaimed as Patch, his Jack Russell, scurried down the lane towards them. Out of the corner of his eye he saw Megan stiffen, and he hastened to reassure her. 'He's very friendly and the ponies are used to him, so there's no need to worry.'

'I'm not. Hello, boy.' She crouched down and the terrier almost leapt into her arms in excitement. He tried to lick her face and she laughed. 'What's his name?'

'Patch.'

She glanced up at him and Nathan caught her amused smile.

'It's because he's got this brown bit over his eye,' he explained. 'I know it's not very original.'

'Who cares?' she said. 'As long as you're happy with it, that's all that matters. We were going to have a Jack Russell,' she said, her tone wistful. 'We even went as far as making an appointment to see some puppies, but Jeremy became ill and...' She sighed. 'In some ways I wish we'd gone ahead and bought one, but it wouldn't have been fair on the dog.' Another sigh. 'It must be nice having him to come home to.' She gave Patch a final cuddle and put him on the ground.

'It is,' Nathan said. 'But he usually goes everywhere with me.'

'What about shopping?'

'I get everything delivered.'

'Meals out?'

'I have pie and chips in the Black Horse now and again, and they allow dogs, so...'

'What about visits to the barber? The dentist? The doctor?'

'I take him with me to the barber, he sits in the car when I go to the dentist and I can't remember the last time I went to the doctor. I'm never ill.'

She looked at him sharply. 'Let's hope you never are.'

'How long was your husband ill for?'

'Long enough.'

'It must have been tough.'

'It's been tougher since he died.'

'I expect it has. Are you going to get yourself a dog?'

'I can't; I'm at work all day.'

'Best you don't, then,' he agreed. 'You can always borrow this one.'

'You mean, like walk him?'

'If you want. He doesn't need much walking, though – he gets plenty of exercise around the stables. You ought to see him and Petra's dog playing together. It makes me tired just looking at them.' They reached the yard and he added, 'Tango goes in this stall here, and Parsnip in that one.'

He watched to make sure Megan was okay, then he turned his attention to his own ponies, grateful for a chance to be on his own for a few minutes. He couldn't recall the last time he'd chatted to a total stranger as much as he'd talked to Megan. But it wasn't his garrulousness that concerned him – it was the way she made him feel. Unsettled, uncertain, uneasy – and probably a whole lot more words beginning with **un**, if only he could think of them. One word did spring to mind, one which he knew he had to heed, and that was the word **dangerous**.

Because he was in danger of liking her –
and that would never do, would it?

By the time all four animals had been
bedded down it was fully dark and had
begun to rain heavily. Megan, water
glistening in the strands of hair
surrounding her face, hoisted her hood up
over her head, shouted, 'Goodbye, see
you next week!' and made a dash for her
car.

To his astonishment, Nathan was sorry to
see her go.

'Dangerous,' he muttered to himself,
calling Patch to heel. But despite the risk
to his equanimity, he couldn't help looking
forward to next week's riding lesson.

'How did the riding lesson go?' Richard
asked Megan the following Monday when
he phoned her at work. As always when
Megan heard his voice her heart twisted

with renewed pain; he sounded so like Jeremy that some days it hurt to speak to him.

'It was incredibly enjoyable,' she said, glancing into the corridor to check no one was listening to her conversation. She had an office of her own, but her open-door policy meant her door was usually ajar. The rest of the department was open-plan, and the illusion was enhanced by the use of large windows instead of walls. Sometimes she felt as though she was working in a fish tank.

'Petra, the woman who runs the place, is lovely,' she continued. 'She put me on this gentle old mare, and to be honest I was a bit put out because I thought I could handle something with a bit more spirit. But she was right – I haven't ridden in such a long time that it took me a while to regain my confidence.'

'I take it I won't be seeing you in The Horse of the Year Show any time soon?'

His chuckle stole her breath and she swallowed, reminding herself it wasn't Jeremy on the other end of the phone.

'I used to dream of that when I was a girl. Now all I'm dreaming about is being able to sit down without groaning – I'm still aching! I could hardly get out of bed the next morning. It was fun though. I'm glad I went.'

'Good.' She heard the relief in his voice and knew it hadn't been easy for him. As the executor of Jeremy's will he must have dreaded handing her those envelopes and witnessing her grief all over again, as her husband reached out to her from beyond the grave. Richard had his own mourning to endure.

'How do you feel about this being the last envelope?' he asked.

'Abandoned, relieved, sad...when **don't** I feel sad?' she joked ruefully. 'I get why Jeremy organised them, but I'm not sure they helped. In fact, I know they didn't; I miss him as much today as I did the day he died.'

'You were going to miss him, regardless. Would you like me to come over after work?'

Megan would dearly like him to, but she didn't **need** him to. And that was the difference between those early days of inconsolable grief and today. She'd probably have a little cry when she got home (she often did) but she now had ways of coping, and she had learnt not to rely on Richard so much for emotional support.

'Thanks for the offer but I'll be fine. I'm going to make myself some pasta and contemplate what I want to do with the rest of my life,' she said.

'That's...um...some evening. Are you **sure** you don't want me to pop in?'

'I want a dog.'

'Okaaay...' Richard drew the word out and she heard the concern and bewilderment in his voice. He must think she was becoming unhinged, when actually she was seeing clearer than she'd done for years.

'When I was at the stables last week, I realised I don't enjoy my job and I haven't for a while,' she told him.

'What's that got to do with getting a dog?'

She could tell by his tone that he was baffled. 'I'm not **getting** a dog. I **want** a dog – there's a difference.'

'We don't always get what we want,' Richard said.

Didn't she know it. 'I know I have to work, so having a dog would be out of the question, but it made me think what I would do if I had a different job.'

'Get a cat; they're less hassle. You don't have to walk them, for one thing.'

'You're missing the point.'

'Which is?'

'What the hell am I going to do with the rest of my life?'

CHAPTER THREE

'We've only just had Bonfire Night,' Petra grumbled, 'yet here we are, nearly halfway through December. I swear the years are going by faster.'

'That's what happens when you get older,' Nathan said. 'Although you shouldn't be saying something like that at **your** age.'

Petra snorted. Some days she felt like a teenager and others, like today, she felt ninety. 'I'm getting too old for this,' she said, sweeping her arm over the boxes of Christmas decorations.

'You're never too old for Christmas,' Nathan said, and Petra barked out a laugh.

'So says the man who could give Scrooge a run for his money when it comes to festive cheer.'

'I've got plenty of festive cheer,' her handyman said. 'I just don't show it.'

'Humbug,' she retorted. 'Last year you complained constantly about the Christmas songs.'

'They were bloody everywhere,' he said, making her laugh. 'On the telly, on the radio, in the shops, and even—' he glared at her '—in the arena. Did you have to play **Mistletoe and Wine** every five minutes?'

'You can blame Amos for that. If it was up to me, I'd have played **Fairytale of New York**, but Amos wouldn't let me.'

'I can see why. It's not suitable for kids, is it? Where do you want this?' Nathan pointed to the rather large pot containing a rather large tree.

'In the gallery, please.'

'If you've got to play something, I prefer a good old-fashioned carol.'

'Like what? Give me an example.'

'**Away in a Manger** would be nice. Or **Little Donkey**.'

'Good one,' Petra chortled. Nathan might come across as dour, but he had a wicked sense of humour beneath his slightly grim exterior.

Petra had always been ambivalent about Christmas to a certain extent. When she was a child, all she'd wanted for Christmas was a pony. Needless to say she'd never got one, and she'd found it hard to pretend to show enthusiasm for the presents she did receive. It had been ungrateful of her and she realised her parents must have been hurt, but she couldn't do anything about the way she felt – they were unable to give her the only thing she truly wanted, and they knew it. The one shining light of any Christmas was when the family paid a visit to the stables on Muddypuddle Lane, and she was able to get her fix of all things horsey.

Then when she'd moved in with Amos and had taken over the running of the stables, Petra had realised that in some respects Christmas Day was like any other, in that the animals still had to be cared for. Horses came first; unwrapping gifts and having a glass of eggnog or mulled wine came second. And she did mean only one glass, because the animals also needed seeing to in the evening. Besides, trying to deal with a tetchy goat or a pony with an attitude when you had a hangover on Boxing Day wasn't much fun.

She watched Nathan manoeuvre the tractor into position and ease the tines of the forklift attachment away from the pot. It was a delicate job, and needed some muscle at the end to wiggle it into position. Petra was glad Nathan was there to do it. She was perfectly capable of driving a tractor and had moved the Christmas tree into the arena in the past, but this year if Nathan hadn't been around, she didn't think she could have faced it. Maybe next year they'd leave the damned thing where it was and buy a smaller tree.

Satisfied it was in position, she stood back to admire it. 'I feel like leaving it au naturale this year,' she said, not relishing the thought of getting the ladder out and climbing up and down it numerous times in order to decorate it.

Oh, well, it was for the kids and their parents. They expected it, and she had to admit that when it was done it did look lovely. She wanted to finish the trimming up by Thursday afternoon, ready for the weekend classes, and she ran through a mental list of what she had on for today and tomorrow: two beginner classes this evening, and a private lesson tomorrow afternoon with Megan Barnes, followed by a showjumping class an hour afterwards. It should give her enough time to get it all done, especially if she roped Charity into helping. But then, Charity was needed for other things.

Petra acknowledged she needed to employ someone else, but just before Christmas wasn't the best time to advertise a vacancy. Nathan had mentioned it again last week, when Megan had given him a hand to fetch the last of the ponies in after her lesson had ended. Petra had teased him about it because he was never normally as friendly with the clients, and he'd become even more close-lipped than usual, which had led her to wonder if she'd touched a nerve. For most of the parents who brought their children to the stables, he faded into the background. She'd never noticed him speaking to any of them unless he had to though, so it was a surprise to see him happily chatting to Megan.

Did Nathan like her? If so, he wasn't letting on, and Petra wondered how Megan felt about him. He wasn't the most talkative of men, and people often found him rather distant, but Megan seemed to be getting on all right with him.

Petra thought back to the conversation she'd had with Megan's husband nearly two years ago. He'd been direct and lacking in self-pity when he'd told her what he was planning and why, and she'd assured him that no matter how long it took for his widow to book her lessons, she'd honour the payment. It hadn't occurred to Petra that it would take two years, so when Megan Barnes had arrived for her lesson, Petra had assumed her husband had managed to hold out for longer than he'd anticipated, even though Jeremy Barnes had told her he didn't have more than a few weeks to live.

It looked like he'd been right.

His wife was still grieving, but was two years enough to think about having another relationship? And if so, would the woman think of Nathan in that way? Petra would like nothing better than to see Nathan fall in love – as long as the love was reciprocated.

With a huff at her silliness, Petra forced her mind away from matters of the heart (she blamed it on being so loved-up herself, and she simply couldn't imagine being without Harry now), and tried to focus on the task at hand, which was decorating this ridiculously tall tree.

She really didn't feel like it; what she felt like was a nap.

Blimmin' heck, she must be getting old if she was wishing she could take a nap during the day. Maybe she should start taking supplements, or something? Admittedly the last couple of months had been hectic, what with the Halloween Party, then Harry moving into the stables and Faith no longer helping out, but she was only in her early thirties for goodness' sake. As soon as the festivities were out of the way, she'd put an advert in the paper, because the sooner she had another pair of hands around the place, the better!

As Petra began to dig around in one of the many boxes of baubles and tinsel, her thoughts kept returning to Megan, and she wondered if the woman had any regrets about falling in love with a man she was to lose far too soon. Was it better to have had such love in her life, or would she have preferred to have never met him?

Petra pondered her own circumstances as she carefully decorated the tree, and she came to the conclusion that by the time she had realised she was in love, it had been too damned late to do anything about it. All she hoped was that she didn't lose Harry, because now he was in her life, she didn't know how she'd carry on if he disappeared out of it.

'The decorations look great,' Megan said as she did a lap of the arena on a gorgeous horse called Sherbet. Petra was standing in the middle, turning slowly on the spot and giving the occasional reply between issuing instructions.

'Ask her to canter. You'll have to keep her on a short rein, because she might be a bit keen,' Petra advised. 'It took two days to decorate the place. Good, watch your seat, you're starting to get sloppy, and keep those elbows in. That's better.'

Megan tried to maintain an upright posture, but it was far too easy to lean over the animal's neck, which Sherbet interpreted as a request to go faster. Sitting up straight again, Megan gently pulled the horse back, using her hands and her legs, until the canter was more of a rocking horse gait, than a potential headlong rush.

'You are lucky you knew you always wanted to work with horses. I need a change,' Megan said. 'Do something different with my life.' She didn't know why she was confiding in Petra, but for some reason she felt she could talk to her.

'What were you thinking of doing?' Petra asked.

'No idea.' Megan sounded cheerful, but inside she was anything but. Changing jobs would be the last big upheaval in her life for a while, and one which she now recognised was long overdue. If Jeremy hadn't fallen ill, she probably would have taken this step three years ago. But once the cancer was diagnosed, nothing else mattered. And by the time it was all over, she was just grateful she had a job she could slot back into without any fuss. She knew her role inside out, and although it helped keep her occupied during the day and was challenging enough to stop her from dwelling on things (and she'd been very glad of that at the time), she didn't enjoy it any more. When she peered into the future, she couldn't see herself working in the same place in twenty years' time.

The problem was, she didn't know what else she wanted to do instead. Whatever it was, she'd more than likely have to retrain, unless she intended to swap HR for another admin job, which would be pointless. But returning to full-time education was out because she still had bills to pay, and although they weren't extortionate, being without an income for however long it took to complete a course wasn't an option.

'It's going to be tricky to find something else, if you don't know what you want to do,' Petra said, stifling a yawn. 'Sorry, I'm exhausted.'

'Too many late nights?'

'Too many early mornings. The damn cockerel wakes me up at five-thirty every morning.'

'I thought they were supposed to crow at dawn? It doesn't get properly light until eight.'

'I don't think he got the memo,' was Petra's dry response. 'Okay, how do you feel about walking over some poles?'

'Can I?' Megan's eyes lit up. Walking over poles was the first step towards jumping.

'We're not talking about five-foot fences here,' Petra said, going across to the far corner of the arena where all kinds of poles and jumps were kept. She lifted one of the poles and carried it to the middle and dropped it on the ground. 'Ouch!'

'Are you okay?' Megan asked as Petra rubbed the side of her chest.

'Caught myself in the boob,' she said. 'They're bloody sore, too. Who'd be a woman, eh? Men don't know how lucky they are not to have periods.'

Nathan had just opened the door and stepped inside, when he caught the tail end of Petra's grumble, and he promptly did an about-face. 'Oh, I'm out of here!'

Megan grinned. Jeremy never had an issue discussing periods, but some men were averse.

'Come back and help me with this pole,' Petra shouted after him, and after a second his head appeared around the door.

He looked positively terrified.

'Can you set up three poles on the ground, five paces apart? Thanks.' It didn't seem as though Petra was going to take no for an answer.

Megan smiled at him apologetically and mouthed, 'Sorry.'

He shrugged. Then he smiled at her and Megan blinked. Crumbs, he should do that more often. It had transformed him from a slightly po-faced bloke into a man who was rather handsome in a rugged, outdoorsy kind of way.

Nathan was another person who seemed happy in his job, and she envied him. Working at the stables wasn't high-powered and it was hardly likely to make him rich, yet he seemed happy, despite his outward grouchiness.

'Megan was saying she's thinking about changing jobs,' Petra said to him, as he carried the next pole and measured out the correct number of paces before he dropped it in position.

'Oh aye? We could do with a hand here,' he said, giving Petra a pointed look. 'We're a body down.'

Megan saw him wince at the word "body", and she shook her head. It seemed he was unable to avoid mentioning things to do with death. It didn't bother her, but it seemed to bother him.

'I don't think that's the kind of thing Megan had in mind,' Petra said.

'You mean be a stable hand? I'd love to!' Megan giggled when she saw their faces. 'Or I would if I was twenty years younger.

I'm not cut out for humping bales of hay around, or for being outside in the cold and the wet.'

'Fair-weather rider,' Nathan teased.

'Guilty as charged, and I don't mind admitting it. I hate being cold.'

'Yet you want to ride in the snow?'

'It does seem incongruous, doesn't it?' Megan agreed. 'But it's a cherished memory of mine, and one I would love to repeat. Jeremy understood that...' She became pensive, then abruptly snapped out of it. 'Sorry, I didn't mean to kill the mood.'

She saw Nathan wince again. He needed to get over his worry about her feelings she thought, as she first walked Sherbet over the poles, and then trotted her over them.

By the end of the lesson she was aching again, but once more she'd thoroughly enjoyed it and she felt lighter than she'd felt for a very long time. Jeremy, bless him, had known what he was doing. All of the gifts he'd given her had been designed to lift her spirits, or to push her so she didn't get stuck in a rut of grief and longing. This last one, she understood, was a farewell...

She wasn't yet ready to let him go, but she was getting there. He'd always be a big part of her, the best part, but it was nearing the time for her to move on. Life was too precious to waste it in sadness and heartbreak, and she was now beginning to feel able to face it again.

The hard part was almost over – compared to what she'd been through. Deciding what she wanted to do with the rest of her life would be a piece of cake.

Cake? Ah, now, there was a thought...

CHAPTER FOUR

Megan was on her hands and knees, with her head in a cupboard which was crammed with all those things she'd kept because they might come in handy one day but she'd probably never use again if she was being truthful.

Yet today she **was** going to use something from out of there, if only she could find it.

There it was, her cake decorating box. It looked like a toolbox but held everything the budding cake decorator needed.

Although, Megan wasn't so much budding, as lapsed. Years ago, she used to balance the demands of her job by the creativity of designing cakes. She also used to go running, but that wasn't something she was planning on resurrecting any time soon. She didn't think her knees could cope.

Stiffly and with a considerable amount of groaning and pulling herself up by hanging onto the worktop, she got to her feet. Riding had certainly highlighted how unfit she was, and although she was aching slightly less than last week, her muscles continued to protest at the unaccustomed exercise.

Opening the box, Megan broke into a sad smile. She vividly remembered baking Jeremy a cake for his thirtieth birthday and how pleased she'd been with the result. He loved old cars, and she'd made a kind of road out of grey fondant icing which curled around the sides of the cake and across the top. And in the centre of it, she'd modelled a Triumph Spitfire. At least, that was what it was supposed to have been. Anyway, he'd loved it, and she'd gone on to make loads of other cakes over the years for friends and family. Then life had become so much more difficult, and she had slipped the toolbox into the cupboard and it had sat there ever since.

The first thing she needed to do was to bake a cake, and for a while Megan couldn't think what sort, but as Christmas was looming she decided to make a festive one. If it turned out okay, she'd take it to work and let her colleagues devour it.

She'd dropped into the supermarket on the way home from her riding lesson yesterday and had picked up flour, butter, eggs and anything else she needed, so she set about making a simple Victoria sponge with orange-flavoured buttercream filling. It had taken her a few minutes to firstly find her cake tins (under the stairs), rinse and dry them, then remember the quantities of each ingredient. Eventually though, the cakes were rising in the oven and with the delicious aroma wafting up her nose, she thoroughly washed and sorted all her cake decorating equipment before she decided how she wanted to decorate it.

Remembering she had several books on the subject, Megan eventually found them in the attic. She'd put them up there, along with a great many other things when their living room had been repurposed as a bedroom for Jeremy in those final few weeks before he'd died.

Megan hadn't bothered to bring any of it back down, and she'd become used to only seeing the bare bones of the three-piece suite and a few other bits of furniture. It had suited her mood.

Now though, she brought an armful of books down with her, dusted them off, and popped them on the almost empty shelves of the bookcase, which had once held an astonishing and disturbing array of medical equipment and medicines.

The cake decorating books looked lonely all by themselves, and she vowed to return the bookcase to its proper function soon. Now, though, she had a cake cooling on a wire rack and she had to decide what she was going to do with it.

Flicking through the first book she picked up and loving some of the cakes in its pages, she sadly came to the conclusion that she needed to start simple and work her way up to a more complicated design. So she chose a snowman's face for this attempt. It was rather childlike, but she realised she had a better chance of making it look decent, than if she tried a more complex one.

The next two hours were spent happily rolling out sheets of fondant icing to cover the whole cake (white for the snowman's head and face) then messily colouring the rest of the icing to make a green and red hat, which she patterned using the tines of a fork to make it look like woollen material. Then she added a red scarf around the side, and black blobs for the eyes and mouth. She finished it off by using some orange icing which she'd fashioned into a cone shape to represent a carrot for the nose.

It wasn't the most professional cake she'd ever seen, but it wasn't hideous either, and she carefully put it to one side ready to take to work on Monday.

Reluctant to pack everything away – because she had nothing else to do for the rest of the day – she had a go at making some fondant roses, which were more difficult than she remembered, and then she whipped up a batch of royal icing and had a go at piping.

Hmm...that was trickier than she remembered too, she decided, as she stood back and surveyed the designs she'd tried to create.

They weren't the best, she acknowledged, and she wondered if she'd ever been very good at royal icing decorations or whether she was misremembering. Admittedly, she was better with fondant – it was more forgiving and somewhat like modelling with playdough.

Wanting to be good at both and realising it might not be a simple case of practice makes perfect, Megan cleaned up the quite considerable mess she'd made then dug out her tablet.

Always one for recognising the benefits of training, she searched the websites of local colleges and was delighted when she found a ten-week cake decorating course starting after Christmas which took place in the evenings. Not only would she learn new things, but it would also get her out of the house for a few hours.

Megan now had something else in her life to look forward to, and she was starting to feel renewed hope for the future.

But even with a subdued excitement about her new venture slowly starting to build, her thoughts kept returning to the stables on Muddypuddle Lane and the man who had unwittingly piqued her reluctant interest.

Nathan strolled into the Black Horse, sniffing the aroma of beer and chips. It was a heady combination, and he thought he might treat himself to pie and chips to go with his pint of real ale. He'd opened the fridge when he'd got home from work, stared balefully at its contents, then closed the door again. Nothing had appealed to him, so he'd gone to the pub instead. He'd fed Patch of course; the dog ate better and more regularly than his master did, and no doubt he'd cadge a bit of pie from Nathan's plate.

Being the only hostelry in the village, the Black Horse was usually busy, especially

on a Saturday evening and tonight was
no exception.

'All right, Nathan? How's tricks?' Amos
was already there, propping up the bar, a
pint of Guinness in front of him and a set
of darts in his hand. 'Fancy a game?'

'You know I can't play for toffee. Besides,
I need food first.' He signalled for Patch
to sit, then attracted Dave's attention and
ordered a pint and his dinner.

'You're not that bad. I've seen you throw
a decent dart. And you should have eaten
with us – there was plenty to go round.
We had sausage and mash, and the onion
gravy was the tastiest I've made yet,
even if I do say so myself.'

'Maybe I should have,' Nathan replied,
not meaning it. He loved the stables, he
loved Petra and Amos, and he'd taken
quite a liking to Harry, but that didn't
mean he wanted to live in their pockets.

And he was pretty sure they didn't need him hanging around all the time.

He felt a clap on his back and he turned to see Harry squashing in between them. 'Amos is right, his gravy is the best,' Harry said.

Nathan gave him a rueful smile. He'd forgone the offer of an evening meal at the stables (Amos always offered and Nathan nearly always refused) so they didn't have to put up with him after work, yet here they all were in the pub together. Except for one person.

'No Petra tonight?' he asked.

'She didn't feel like it,' Harry said. 'I'm only here because Amos needed dropping off, and I'll only have the one pint so I can pick him up later. I'll finish this—' he nodded at the half-empty glass on the bar '—then I'll go home and spend a couple of hours with Petra. She'll probably be asleep though,' he added regretfully. 'I wish she'd get a move on and employ someone else; she's like the walking dead at the moment with all this extra work.'

'Tell me about it,' Nathan grumbled.

After he'd ordered his meal, he left Amos and Harry at the bar and took a seat at a free table. He was just about to take his second sip of ale, when he noticed who was sitting at the table next to him.

'How is Midnight?' Faith asked. She was cuddling up to her boyfriend Dominic and happiness was shining out of her.

Mind you, he thought, her twin, Charity, looked equally as happy. Timothy, Harry's brother, had his arm around her and was holding her close. They made a lovely couple. To his shame, Nathan felt a little envious – oh to be so young and in love. If only he had his time over again...

'Your horse is fine,' he assured her.

'He's not my horse anymore,' she reminded him, her face sad. She clicked her fingers and Patch got up to allow her to fondle his floppy ears.

'He'll always be your horse in here,' Nathan said, and tapped his chest.

'That's a lovely thing to say,' Charity cried. 'I'll have to remember that when one of the residents is upset about the loss of their pet. Brian was upset again today because he remembered his dog has had to be rehomed. He's got dementia,' she explained, 'and some days he thinks he still owns the dog and other days he remembers that he had to give him up.'

'Aw, bless,' Faith said, and Nathan saw the genuine sympathy in the girl's eyes. He knew it must have been hard for her to sell Midnight, but horses weren't like dogs – as long as their owners were good to them, most of them didn't seem particularly bothered who they belonged to.

He felt for Brian even though he'd never met him. He'd be devastated if he had to give Patch up. The dog was a huge part of his life and as far as Nathan was concerned anyone who didn't like his dog wasn't welcome.

Abruptly, an image of Megan crouching down to gather Patch into her arms popped into his mind and his stomach did an odd roll. Flippin' heck, he should have eaten before he came out. He was starving and Patch, who was lying at his feet, whined as though he sensed his master's mood.

'What do you think?' Charity asked him.

'Sorry, what?' He'd been so lost in his thoughts he had no idea what she was talking about.

'About taking Gerald to the care home.'

Nathan blinked at her. 'Did you say, **Gerald**?'

'Yes.'

'To the care home?'

'That's right. I'm sure the residents would love to see him, especially on Christmas Eve. You're okay with that, aren't you, Amos?'

Amos nodded. Harry appeared bemused. Nathan didn't blame him: he was rather bemused himself.

'Donkey poo and carpets don't mix,' Nathan pointed out.

'He can come as far as the reception area – that has wooden flooring. We should be able to fit everyone in, if we squash the chairs together. Amos can lead him in and we can have panniers on him for the presents.'

'Panniers.' Nathan was close to speechless. 'Where on earth are you going to get panniers from?

'I'm sure we can make some.'

'Good luck.'

'I'll help,' Timothy said, and Faith piped up, 'So will I.'

Nathan pursed his lips. 'You'll have to run it past Petra,' he said, and he wasn't certain she'd agree. It was one thing taking a small dog into a care home, but it was another thing altogether to take a donkey for a visit. Still, it was a lovely idea and would make Christmas Eve quite magical for the residents, so he vowed to do everything he could to help make it happen. 'If she says yes, count me in,' he said.

Charity leant across the space between his table and hers, and planted a big kiss on his cheek. 'I knew I could count on you.'

'Get off,' he grumbled, but secretly he was pleased. It was nice to feel useful and it was even nicer to feel appreciated. But even as he mulled over the practicalities of getting Gerald from the stables to the care home, his thoughts kept returning to Megan and the sadness in her eyes.

CHAPTER FIVE

Megan used to adore Christmas. Even as little as three years ago, she used to love immersing herself in the festivities and she enjoyed everything about it, from carefully choosing and wrapping each present, to baking mince pies and making her own mulled wine. Then there were all the parties and the socialising, plus visiting their respective families, and afterwards winding down with cosy nights in front of the TV drinking mugs of hot chocolate and stuffing their faces with marshmallows.

Until it had all changed; and now she dreaded Christmas. There were only eight days to go until she would wake up on Christmas morning filled with indescribable sadness and an ache in her chest, which wouldn't leave until everyone was back at work and life had returned to normal. Or what passed for normal now that Jeremy was gone.

Megan didn't anticipate that this second festive season without her husband would be any better than the first. If anything it might be worse, because she knew what to expect.

At least she'd have something to take her mind off it this year for a while, because when she was making and decorating cakes she was fully immersed in what she was doing. So far, she'd made three cakes and had also created a complete nativity scene out of fondant icing. What she was going to do with it, she had yet to decide. But she had brought one of the cakes with her to the stables to give to Petra and the others. Megan would never eat it all by herself and it seemed a shame to waste it. This one was the best so far, and she was rather proud of it. Three rotund reindeers in decreasing sizes sat on the top, roped together with a harness, and pulling a sledge with a sack of presents on it. The presents were small and had been fiddly to make, but now they were done they looked quite good, she thought.

But when she stuck her head around the door to the arena to let Petra know she'd arrived, she was taken aback to see Nathan readying the horses, especially since he had a helmet on and was wearing proper riding boots and not the steel toe-capped footwear he usually had on his feet.

'Hi, I, um, brought you a cake.' She held up the box. 'Not you personally, you understand: it's for everyone at the stables. The human occupants, I mean, ha ha.' She was rambling. No wonder Nathan was staring at her oddly. 'Shall I put it in the office? I'll get a helmet while I'm there.' She hesitated. 'Are you going out for a ride?'

'I am.' He turned away to check the girth on a chestnut thoroughbred stallion, who looked to be a bit of a handful.

'That's nice.' As much as she'd enjoyed her lessons in the arena, she longed to be outdoors – there was something very uplifting about riding across fields and hillsides. 'I'll get my helmet and wait for Petra, shall I?' Her lesson was due to start any minute, so she knew Petra wouldn't be far away.

'No need, I'm taking you out today.'

'You're taking my lesson?'

'No, I'm taking you out for a hack.' He glanced around at her and noticed her shocked reaction.

'You are?'

'Which bit are you unsure about? Me taking you out? Or going out at all? Petra said you were ready for a gentle ride up onto the moors, but if you don't want to—'

'I want to!' Excitement surged through her, and she couldn't wait to mount up. Hastily she hurried into the office, popped the cake on the desk and scribbled a note, then grabbed her hat.

She was back in the arena in a trice.

Nathan was standing at Sherbet's head. 'Do you need a hand getting on her? I can take her over to the mounting block, if you want.'

The mounting block was a large lump of chiselled rock in the shape of two steps, and Megan was tempted, but what she really wanted to do was to try to get on by herself. She'd been doing all kinds of stretches to aid her flexibility and she wanted to see if they were working.

'I can manage,' she said, taking the reins from him and putting her left foot in the stirrup. One bounce, then another, and she hoisted herself into the saddle, ignoring the way the mare turned to look at her ungainly antics with a curious stare.

'Yes,' she cried, and earned another curious look, this time from Nathan.

As soon as she was settled, Nathan came around to the side of her horse and checked both stirrup lengths. Megan moved her leg to allow him better access to the straps, but when he accidentally brushed her shin with his hand, a surge of heat shot up her leg. She bit back a gasp; it was a very long time since a man had touched her. Her father and Richard didn't count, neither did her doctor or dentist. Nathan was a relative stranger, and although he was simply doing his job, she felt weirdly embarrassed. Her reaction didn't help, either.

'Try them now,' he said, stepping back, and she was pleased he hadn't noticed how weirdly she was behaving.

She slid her feet back into the stirrups and raised herself out of the saddle. 'They're fine,' she said, eager to get going so he didn't see the blush spreading across her cheeks.

'Good.' He walked over to the stallion and mounted up. 'Ready?'

'Absolutely.' She urged Sherbet forward and the mare fell in behind the other horse. 'Where's Patch?' she wondered.

'Sleeping in front of the fire – him and Queenie both. They're not daft.'

Megan wondered whether Nathan thought she was daft for wanting to go riding on this cold, glum day. She gazed at his back, straight and tall on the back of his horse. 'What's the horse's name? Is he yours?'

'He's Petra's horse and his name is Hercules. She doesn't let anyone else ride him, apart from me and Harry.'

'I'm not complaining or anything, but I just wondered why Petra isn't taking me out.'

'Christmas.'

'Ah, I see. It's a busy time of year for everyone.'

It used to be a busy time of year for her too, but not any more.

Megan hadn't gone to a party since Jeremy's diagnosis, and neither had she gone out for a meal, or for drinks after work.

Nathan gave a noncommittal grunt, and she suddenly got the feeling it wasn't a very busy time of year for him either.

'Do you work much over Christmas?' she asked, wondering if he got any time off at all.

'I have to – the animals don't look after themselves.'

'Petra relies on you a lot, doesn't she?'

Megan saw his shoulders lift in a shrug. 'Running a riding school is a lot of work for one person. Amos does his best, but he's got to be careful because of his angina. He helps in other ways, like keeping the house going and doing all the paperwork.'

'Do you like your job?' she asked, as he angled his horse sideways up to a gate and lifted the latch. What was it with her need to know if other people enjoyed their jobs? Was she trying to justify what she was thinking of doing, or was she trying to give herself a reason to stay in a job she disliked – hoping if no one else was happy in their work there would be little incentive for her to change career.

'I love my job,' he said, asking Hercules to back up so he could open the gate.

Sherbet walked through, and Megan pulled her up to wait for Nathan. His answer didn't surprise her; she'd already got the impression he liked what he did.

'Harry loves his, too,' Nathan said, passing her to lead the way.

Megan took a deep breath of extremely chilly air, glad she'd worn an extra fleece under her coat and hadn't left her scarf in the car. At least it didn't look like rain, as the sky was cloudless, the weak sun low in the sky. The shortest day would soon be upon them, and dusk wouldn't be far off by the time today's ride was over.

'You've got to love animals to be able to work with them,' Nathan was saying as the path widened and he slowed to allow her to walk alongside.

She asked, 'Did you always want to work with horses?'

'I'm from farming stock,' he said, 'so I've grown up with sheep and cows, dogs and chickens. I've worked on farms all my life. My brother and his family still run the family farm.'

'Didn't you want to run it?'

'We don't rub along too good. I'm better off working for someone else. Besides, he's got his own family – my nephews are grown up now and they help run it with him.'

'What about you? Do you have a family?'

'Wife and kids? No.' His voice was terse, and she wondered what had happened to him in the past. 'Have you got any kids?'

'No. We always meant to, but it wasn't a driving ambition, and then when Jeremy became ill it went off the radar completely.'

They rode in silence for a while, and she sarcastically congratulated herself for being able to kill the mood.

'What do you do for a living?' he asked after a while.

'I work in HR.'

'Do you like your job?'

'Not really.'

'Why do you do it?'

'I sort of fell into it after university. I'd been doing some admin work for an agency to gain some experience, and saw a vacancy in the HR department of the council, and it all started from there.'

'Why do you do it?' he repeated, and she gave him a sharp glance.

'I know my job inside out – I could probably do it standing on my head – and the money is good. To be honest, staying there was the easiest thing to do.'

'What about now?'

Megan shot him another look; he was incredibly astute. 'I don't know,' she admitted.

'I'm not the best person to be giving career advice,' he said, 'but all I can say is, life's too short to stay in a job you don't like. You spend the biggest part of your week at work...'

'I want to make cakes,' she blurted.

He glanced at her. 'So why not do it?'

'It's easier said than done.'

'No, it's not.'

'You don't understand; I've got bills to pay, a car to run.'

'Haven't we all? But you cut your coat according to your cloth.'

Megan frowned; this ride wasn't turning out to be as relaxing as she'd hoped. But he did have a point, and hadn't she been thinking the exact same thing herself, otherwise why was she asking people whether they liked their jobs, and why had she signed up for a cake decorating course. Deep down she knew she wanted it to be more than a hobby.

So what was stopping her?

Her own fear, that's what.

Yet, Nathan was right. She didn't have a mortgage (they'd saved hard to pay it off) and she had some savings. And she could certainly trim quite a bit off her monthly outgoings. She didn't need the satellite TV package she was currently paying for (she always switched the TV on every evening, but if anyone asked her what she'd watched she wouldn't be able to remember). She could sell her car and buy a smaller one which was cheaper to run. She had no inclination to go on holiday (on her own? no thanks!), and she had more clothes than she could possibly wear. So did she need such a well-paying job?

'I'm looking forward to trying your cake,' Nathan said.

Megan grimaced. 'Please be honest with me. If it's awful I prefer you to tell me.' She leant forward in the saddle, putting most of her weight onto the horse's front legs to help the mare stumble up a particularly steep and rocky section of the path. It was instinctive and she was pleased she'd remembered to do it without having to think about it.

He nodded slowly. 'Just as long as you don't get upset.'

'I promise I won't.' She probably would, but she'd do her utmost not to show it. 'I used to bake and decorate cakes all the time, but life got in the way.'

'It has a habit of doing that.'

'I've signed up for a cake decorating course at the college, starting in January. If that goes well, maybe I'll have a serious think about my future.'

'It sounds to me like you've already had a serious think.'

It was true. She had. She just needed to see whether she had the skill to make beautiful cakes, and whether anyone would want to buy them. For a while she could do the cake decorating alongside her day job, because she had nothing else to occupy her time in the evenings and at weekends. Maybe nothing would come of it, but she decided to give it a go. She would only regret it if she didn't.

'My husband should have bought me a cake decorating course instead of riding lessons,' she said, and was bemused when Nathan firmly shook his head.

'Did Jeremy ride?' he asked.

'No. I don't think he'd ever been on the back of a horse.'

'I suspected as much. I think he gave you the perfect gift – for **you**.'

She smiled. 'You're biased.'

'I might be, but the lessons are for you and you alone. They weren't because it was something the two of you enjoyed together, and your husband was reminding you of it. He was reminding you of what **you** loved to do. Look, I never knew Jeremy, but please don't shout at me if I suggest he bought you the lessons in order for you to reconnect to who you used to be before…'

'He died?'

'Yes.'

Maybe he had, at that. For some reason being on the back of a horse had not only reminded her of the past when she was young and free and heartwhole, it had also made her think of the future, and how she was going to live it without Jeremy in it. But her thoughts weren't panicked, desolate ones, and she now found herself more open and willing to move forwards.

It was a scary and daunting thing, and she didn't just mean her potential career change. She was referring to finally facing a future without Jeremy and opening her heart and mind to new possibilities.

'I'm sure you're right,' she said. Trust Jeremy to have been so thoughtful, and for him to know what she needed even though she hadn't known it herself until now.

She just had to get through Christmas, then she'd attack her future head on.

Sherbet kicked a loose stone, bringing Megan back to the present. Here she was, out on her first real ride in twenty-five years, and she was so far in the past that she wasn't enjoying the present.

Hercules stopped and her mare halted. Nathan pointed down into a little valley cut out of the rock by a small fast-flowing tumbling brook running through the bottom of it. She'd been so engrossed in her thoughts she'd hardly been aware of her surroundings, but when Megan looked to where he was pointing, she inhaled sharply in wonder.

'Oh,' she breathed, her eyes wide in awe, because where the water had eaten into the ground it had left a bank of overhanging rock, soil and grass, and dangling from the overhang were hundreds of icicles. Some were as tall as she, others were less than an arm length, but all of them were totally unexpected and utterly magical.

Once again she thanked Jeremy, but this time she was also grateful to another man, a man who had come into her life unwanted and unbidden but one whom she wanted to get to know on a much deeper level – if only she'd let herself.

Her eyes brimming with unshed tears at the beauty before her, she caught Nathan's eye, and when the burst of attraction cascaded over her, she welcomed it. Maybe she was ready to embrace life again, and maybe, just maybe, Nathan might be the man to help her do it.

Nathan's phone pinged in his pocket and he scrabbled around for it, smiling when he read the message, and announced, 'Amos says he's got a pan of hot chocolate on the go, and a slice of your cake for when we get back. I'll see to the horses while you go into the house and have a warm.' He didn't feel the cold much because he was used to it, but he reckoned Megan must be freezing. It was bitter out on the bare hillside without any trees to deflect the bite of the wind.

'Oh, I don't know,' she said. 'I ought to go home.'

'It's a tradition,' he told her. 'Anyone out on a day like this gets to warm up with a hot drink beside the Aga before they leave.'

'If you're sure?' She still sounded doubtful.

'I'm sure.'

'What about you?'

'I'll have a slice later.'

'You must be frozen, too.'

'I'm not so bad. Anyway, the horses need seeing to before I can think about my own comfort.'

He glanced back at her to see her chewing her lips, which were reddened by the cold and starting to look chapped. He nearly offered her his lip balm, but he thought it was too intimate. If she had been Petra or Charity, he wouldn't have hesitated – needs must, and all that. But he didn't know this woman well enough, and he thought she might take it the wrong way. After all, sharing lip balm wasn't exactly hygienic, although to be fair it was in a small tin and not the stick variety.

'Can I help?' she asked. 'Two pairs of hands make light work.'

'I couldn't ask you to do that.'

'You didn't ask. I offered.'

It was his turn to hesitate. When Petra had asked him if he'd mind taking Megan out for a ride, his heart had missed a beat. Scared of his reaction at the thought of being alone with her for a whole hour, he'd almost said no. Now his hesitation was because he so desperately wanted to say yes; it would mean at least another twenty minutes in her company without anyone else around.

But he was also fearful of his growing feelings towards her. Having no idea how to control them, spending more time with her than was strictly necessary probably wasn't the best idea.

'Okay, then,' he said, and frowned. That wasn't what he'd intended to say, but the words had slipped from his lips without any input from his brain.

With a clatter, the horses trotted up the lane and into the yard, heading eagerly for their stalls, and Nathan slid from the saddle almost before Hercules came to a halt. He hurried over to Sherbet and took a hold of her bridle, guessing Megan's fingers would be frozen.

'If you open that stall there and this one here, we'll get them inside before taking their tack off.'

Megan dismounted, her movements stiff, and she hobbled towards the first loose box and slid the bolt across, then opened the other one.

'Take Sherbet,' he said, handing her the reins. 'There's a brush already in there – you only need to do where the saddle was – and her rug is there, too.'

He watched to make sure she was okay, then he turned his attention to Hercules. Having had far more practice, Nathan was done before Megan, so he called to tell her he was making up a couple of buckets of feed. By the time he'd done that she had finished her task.

For a brief moment they watched the horses tucking into their supper, then Megan shivered and he hastened to get her into the house and out of the increasingly cold wind.

'Blimey, it's bitter out there,' he announced as he showed her into the kitchen. Patch leapt up and jumped into Nathan's arms, his backside waggling with the force of his waggy tail as he uttered little whimpers of joy.

Amos was stirring a saucepan full of brown liquid and the enticing smell of chocolate hovered in the air. Petra and Harry were also there, mugs in hands, and so was Timothy.

Nathan made the introductions, even though he felt it wasn't his place to do so, and once everyone had said hello, he buried his nose in his dog's warm coat and cuddled him close.

'They reckon we might have a spot of snow before Christmas,' Amos said.

'It's cold enough,' Timothy said. 'I was on a farm doing TB testing this afternoon, and I swear the temperature has dropped about ten degrees.'

Petra pulled out a chair for Megan and indicated she should take a seat. With a wink at Nathan, Petra pulled out the one next to Megan and dared him to refuse to sit down.

Aware of everyone's eyes on him, Nathan carefully kept his face blank as he dropped into it, still holding onto Patch, who immediately jumped down and clambered onto Megan's lap and demanded attention.

'Would you like marshmallows in yours?' Amos asked Megan.

'Yes, please.'

'You'd better take your coat off, else you won't feel the benefit of it when you go outside,' Petra said. 'Same goes for you, Nathan.'

Nathan shrugged off his coat, and when Megan removed hers he held out his hand for it, using the act of hanging it up on the rack by the door as an excuse to move away from her. As well as the smell of hot chocolate, he'd detected a heavenly scent of perfume and it was making his head spin. Or was that due to the heat of the kitchen? With the Aga going and so many people crammed into it, it was stifling, and he felt his cheeks growing warm.

'Thank you.' Megan took the mug Amos held out to her, wrapped her hands around it and took a sip. 'Mmm, this is delicious.'

'Have a piece of your cake,' Amos said. 'Sorry, but I've already cut into it. Petra couldn't wait to try it.'

'Did you make this?' Harry asked, looking at it.

Megan nodded.

'It's very good, and I love the reindeer.'

Petra grinned at her. 'Thanks for bringing it, it's lovely. You ought to go into business.'

Megan's face glowed, and Nathan thought she might be embarrassed by the compliment, although she looked pleased, too. 'I might just do that,' she said, not meeting anyone's eye.

With his mouth full, Timothy said, 'It's the best cake I've had for ages. Is it too late to order one for Christmas?'

Megan reddened. 'Oh, I don't—'

'You **do**,' Nathan interjected, and Megan stared at him in surprise for a moment. Then her eyes widened and she nodded slowly.

'Erm, no, it's not too late,' she said. 'If you give me your email address, I can send over some ideas, or you can let me know what you want?'

Timothy took out his phone and once they'd swapped numbers, he sent her a message with his email address. 'I'm going to give it to Charity's mum – she's invited me for Christmas lunch.'

'I thought you'd be having lunch with us?' Amos said. 'Harry is, and so is Nathan.'

'I am?' Nathan wasn't surprised – he had Christmas lunch at the stables every year – but he'd yet to be formally invited, so he hadn't taken it for granted he would be this year, especially now Harry had moved in.

'You are,' Amos said, his voice firm.

'Anyway, nice as this is, that's not the reason I called in,' Timothy said. 'I just wanted to warn you that there's been a spate of horse thefts in the area, and to be extra vigilant.'

'Petra is always vigilant, aren't you Petra?' Harry said. 'Petra?' He nudged her. 'Petra.'

'Hmph?'

'You were fast asleep,' he said, with a loving smile. 'You're going to have to place an advert for a stable hand soon because you're burning the candle at both ends. I'm not sure how much longer you can keep this up.'

Petra yawned and stretched. 'I didn't realise how much I relied on Faith. Charity's brilliant too, but she's having to do extra shifts at the care home because there are so many staff off with colds, so we're almost two people down, not one. I suppose I'm going to have to pull my finger out and get something sorted. Should I put an ad in the post office window? And what should I say in it?'

'I can help, if you like,' Megan said, and everyone turned to look at her. This time she didn't blush, and Nathan assumed it was because she was on firmer footing with this type of thing, and more confident of her abilities.

Petra stared at her. 'Of course, you're in human resources.'

'That's right. I've placed more adverts than I've had hot dinners. I can help you write it and suggest where you should advertise it. I assume you have a job description?'

Petra's eyes were wide and she shook her head. 'Should I have?'

'It helps. You'll also need to consider hours of work, salary, holiday entitlement, and so on.'

'Yikes.' Petra glanced at Nathan. 'I didn't give you a job description.'

'You don't give me any holidays, either,' Nathan joked. 'It's lucky I know you so well.'

Petra sighed. 'Okay, thanks Megan. It looks like I'll have need of your services.'

'Have a think about what the hours are, et cetera, and let me know, and I'll put an advert together for you. What start date are you thinking of? I doubt you'll get anyone this close to Christmas, and anyway, you need time to interview and to obtain references.'

'I've never interviewed anyone in my life. Is it strictly necessary?'

'You'll want to make sure they fit in at the stables,' Harry pointed out.

'And it doesn't have to be anything formal,' Timothy added. 'A big part of my interview at the vet practice consisted of dealing with that morning's surgery. Someone brought in a tarantula.'

'What was wrong with it?'

'Dehydration.'

'Really?'

'Yep. He was lethargic and shrivelled.'

Megan visibly shuddered and Nathan felt like doing the same. He didn't mind spiders, but tarantulas were too big for his liking.

'The advert could go out immediately after Christmas, with the aim of interviewing the second week of January,' Megan said, and Nathan was pleased she was taking charge. He had a feeling that left to her own devices, Petra would struggle along, getting more and more worn out because she didn't like the non-horsey side of the business.

'I can't believe it's only a week to Christmas,' Nathan said, thinking this might be a golden opportunity to bring up the subject of Gerald and the care home. 'I, erm, that is... Charity...'

'Gerald?' Petra interrupted.

'You know?'

'Amos told me there was something afoot. Or should I say, ahoof?'

'You don't mind?'

'As long as you're the one who accompanies him, and you clean up his poo; and make sure he doesn't knock anyone over because I don't think I'm insured to take donkeys into care homes.'

Nathan caught Megan's confused expression. Timothy also looked mystified, so Nathan explained. 'Charity thought it might be a nice idea to take Gerald, the donkey, along to the care home on Christmas Eve. Amos dresses up as Santa every year, and there's usually a cheery festive atmosphere.'

'What a lovely thing to do,' Megan enthused.

'You're going to need some help,' Petra said to Nathan. 'I would lend you Harry, but if both you and Amos are going to be in the village, I'll need a hand here.'

Timothy pulled a face. 'I'm on call over most of the Christmas period,' he said. 'I could help but there's no guarantee I'll be there for the whole thing.'

'I don't mind giving you a hand,' Megan offered.

'Great idea. That's settled. Megan can help with Gerald,' Petra declared.

Nathan shot Megan a sharp look. The eagerness in her voice had made him pause, and he was startled to see her glowing. He didn't think it was solely to do with the warmth of the kitchen and neither did he think it was due to embarrassment. He was astonished at how different she now looked, compared to the drab withdrawn woman he'd met three weeks ago. Along with the colour in her cheeks, there was a bit of life about her.

When his heart missed a beat and his stomach did a slow roll as desire surged through him, he was abruptly glad Christmas was fast approaching and he wouldn't see her for a couple of weeks. It was best he put some distance between them, because he wasn't interested in having a woman in his life, and he was pretty sure she didn't want another man.

Not just yet anyway. But the thought of her being with someone else gave him an unaccustomed pang of jealousy.

That's enough, he said to himself. He needed to keep his distance. Once Christmas Eve was out of the way he needn't see her again. Petra would no doubt take her for the remaining two lessons, then that would be the end of it. He vowed to stay out of her way until her last lesson was done and dusted, because she was far too disturbing for his peace of mind.

Megan wasn't at all sure why she had offered to help with the donkey on Christmas Eve, or what help she could possibly give, apart from some moral support, and she wondered what possessed her to offer. She'd already offered her HR skills, so hadn't she done enough? It wasn't as though she owed the stables anything.

But she had felt included and part of something whilst she was in Petra's kitchen, and when she'd returned home and had a chance to mull things over as she sat quietly in her living room with a glass of wine in her hand and soft music playing in the background, she realised what it was – she'd felt as though she belonged. Which was ridiculous, because she'd only met them less than a month ago.

The strange thing was, she felt like she'd known Petra for far, far longer, and Nathan, too. Despite the shortness of their acquaintance, she was beginning to feel as though they were old friends. Heck, she'd told both Petra and Nathan about her misgivings about her job, and she'd even confided in them her desire to make and design cakes. Not only that, but she'd also given them one of her attempts. And they'd all appeared to enjoy it.

Not that she'd thought anyone at the stables would be so mean as to say they didn't like it (she might ask Petra to be brutally honest with her sometime in the future – although not yet) and Harry's younger brother, Timothy, had even asked her to make a cake for him. Jeremy would have been so proud of her.

She wasn't sure how she felt about baking and decorating a cake for a stranger – nervous, excited, apprehensive... Things were moving too fast: one minute she'd been grumbling about her job and wishing she had the courage to do something else, and the next minute she was signed up for a course and had her first commission.

When Nathan stepped in just as she was about to protest that she didn't make cakes for other people and he'd told her she did, she'd felt a rare pride and confidence that she could do this. His simple 'You do,' had given her the courage to say yes to Timothy. Now though she didn't know whether to be grateful to him or annoyed.

She did know one thing however (and it terrified her more than being paid to bake a cake for someone she didn't know) and that was she felt an increasingly strong attraction for Nathan. After her initial disquiet about him accompanying her on the ride in place of Petra, Megan had soon felt glad and, as the hour had ticked by, she'd not wanted the hack to end. So much so, she'd prolonged it by offering to help him put the horses to bed, and then sharing a hot chocolate with him and the others in the stable's kitchen.

She had to admit she liked Nathan a lot. Far more than she wanted to, or felt she should. Not only did she feel she was betraying Jeremy – and that was awful – but Nathan hadn't given her the slightest hint he viewed her as anything more than a client.

Feeling suddenly deflated and lost, she slumped back in her armchair and wished with all her heart she could speak to her husband. Her longing for the man she had vowed to spend the rest of her life with rose up like a tidal wave and crashed over her.

'Why did you have to leave me, Jeremy? Why?' she whispered into the still air, grief clawing at her with sharp talons.

Knowing that the best thing to do was to ride it out and not try to fight it, she nevertheless couldn't stop herself from phoning Richard, because the sound of his voice was the closest she was going to get to hearing her husband's.

 'Oh, hi, Sonja, I, um, is Richard there?' Megan adored Richard's wife and the two women got on well, but it was Richard's voice she needed to hear.

'Hi, Meg, he's out, sorry. Is there anything I can help with, or did you just ring up for a chat?'

Disappointed, Megan tried to lighten up, not wanting her dismal mood to drag Sonja down. 'I was at a bit of a loose end, so I thought I'd ring for a chat.'

'Will I do?'

'Of course, you will,' Megan cried, not wanting to be rude. 'Are you ready for Christmas?'

'Nope. I never am – you know me, I'll still be running around like a headless chicken on Christmas Eve. Are you sure you won't come to us? We'd love to have you.'

'I know, and thanks for the offer. I would love to come to you, too, but I'm going to my parents. They're flying out to Spain for a couple of months immediately after Christmas, so I won't see them for ages. Lucky things.' She suspected they would have gone at the beginning of December but for her, and she felt guilty she was inadvertently spoiling their plans. Then a wave of self-pity engulfed her for being so pathetic and needy, which meant they felt they couldn't leave her on her own over the festive season, even though she would have preferred to forget Christmas was happening. How could she celebrate it without Jeremy? This Christmas, like last year, was something to be endured until it was over.

Sonja said, 'Lucky things! I wish I could disappear off to the sun for a couple of months. Come see us on Boxing Day, instead.'

'Definitely. I'll look forward to it.'

'Liar.'

'Sonja...' Megan was dismayed that her sister-in-law could see through her so easily and she worried she'd upset her. It was the last thing she wanted to do after all the support she'd given her.

'You don't have to pretend,' Sonja said. 'I understand how hard it is for you. It's hard for Richard, too. But we love seeing you.'

'Even when I'm a miserable cow?'

'Even then.' Sonja's soft laughter carried over the airwaves.

They chatted for a bit and Megan enthused about her riding lessons. But maybe she'd mentioned Nathan's name once too often because Sonja abruptly said, 'You like Nathan, don't you?'

'No! Whatever gave you that idea?'

'I don't know – female intuition? And don't sound so shocked. It's a perfectly normal thing to do.'

'No one can replace Jeremy.'

'Of course they can't. But that doesn't mean to say you need to be on your own for the next forty years.'

'Gosh, that sounds so depressing.' That Megan might live one half of her life like Queen Victoria – in a perpetual state of mourning – was a sobering image.

'That's what might happen if you don't give yourself permission to love again,' Sonja said. 'Does he like you?'

Megan said, 'He hardly knows I exist, so it's all hypothetical. Anyway, even if he did fancy me, I can't betray Jeremy.' The guilt she felt at having even the tiniest of feelings for another man was already crippling. Imagine how much worse it would be if she kissed him.

'Would you feel like that if it was you who had died and Jeremy was the one left on his own?' Sonja pointed out.

'That's too awful to contemplate. I'd hate for him not to be happy again.' Megan was adamant. She ignored the stab of pain she felt as the words in his final letter to her slipped into her mind. He'd said the same thing to her – that he hoped she'd move on and find love and happiness again. But how could she?

Echoing her thoughts, Sonja asked, 'Don't you deserve to be happy?'

'But what if I fall in love and he dies?' The thought escaped her before she'd fully formulated it. It wasn't something she'd consciously considered, but now the idea had been spoken she realised how true it was. Was that the real reason she was holding back? She'd been telling herself it was too soon, that she'd lost the love of her life and would never find another, that she would be fine on her own – but were all these things mere excuses because she was terrified she would fall in love again and risk heartache for a second time?

'He **will** die – that's a given. We all will. But it shouldn't stop you from loving someone,' Sonja argued.

'I couldn't keep Jeremy alive,' Megan wailed, the ache in her chest so fierce she thought she might die from it.

'Oh sweetie, no one could.'

'But what if I'd noticed he was ill sooner?' I should have realised—'

'Stop! You can't go on torturing yourself like this. What happened to Jeremy was tragic and awful, but you have to stop blaming yourself.'

Megan was unable to say anything, the words catching in her throat and choking her.

'This Nathan has got you in a right tizzy, hasn't he?' Sonja asked, after a moment.

Sonja was more perceptive than Megan gave her credit for; Nathan **had** got her in a tizzy. She wasn't sure she liked it, but her sister-in-law was right. She didn't want to spend the rest of her life in hopeless despondency.

Maybe she **could** allow herself to love again? To have a relationship? It wouldn't be with Nathan, but at least she could stop beating herself up over finding him attractive and enjoying his company.

She could consider it a trial run for getting out in the world again and one day, when she was finally ready, perhaps she **would** fall in love again.

CHAPTER SIX

Nathan usually felt ambivalent about Christmas Eve. On the one hand, he used to think it was the most magical part of the festive season, especially when he was a child, and sometimes he was able to recall his intense feelings of excitement and joy. On the other hand, it highlighted his aloneness like no other time of the year.

Today, when he'd finished at the stables and he and Patch had returned home, he felt a deep sense of anti-climax when he opened his front door only to be confronted by a cold, dark house and the silence within. As always, he immediately lit a fire and turned the lights and the telly on, so his cottage was soon warm and cosy, but he was unable to dispel that initial impression.

Suddenly, he was glad he was going out tonight. He liked a bit of carol singing even though he was tone deaf, and it would be nice to be around people for a change. There was something about Christmas that disturbed his usual acceptance of being alone.

Nathan had returned to the stables to collect the donkey and he'd just given Gerald a good brushing down and was making sure his halter was sitting right when he heard a car drive up the lane, and a frisson of anticipation ran down his spine.

'Give over,' he muttered, cross with himself. Megan wasn't coming to see **him** – she was here to help with the donkey, and possibly because she'd be on her own too. He didn't know what made him think that, because she'd mentioned family briefly when they'd been on their ride so he knew she wasn't alone in the world, but he got the impression she was lonely nevertheless.

His heart went out to her, and to Amos, as well. This time of year wasn't easy if you'd lost someone you loved, and both of them had lost their spouses. Nathan remembered Amos's wife as a warm, giving lady, and he knew Amos must be feeling her loss even after all these years.

Nathan heard Megan's car door slam and the sound of her quick footsteps across the yard, and he took a moment to compose himself before he ventured out of Gerald's stall. Patch had raced on ahead, eager to greet her. The little dog, although friendly with everyone, had taken a particular liking to Megan.

'Hi,' she said when she saw him, and he was struck anew by her prettiness. Good cheekbones and clear skin, combined with a spring in her step made her appear younger than she was. Although only five years older than her, Nathan felt ancient in comparison. Even if she was ready to "put herself out there", Megan wouldn't want to do so with him. What could he offer her?

'All right?' he replied. 'Amos is just fetching the horsebox, then we can load the donkey into it. You might as well wait in the warm.' He jerked his head towards the house.

'I'm okay to wait out here. We'll probably be glad of some fresh air by the time we're done at Honeymead. It looks lovely. I drove past it on the way here. They've pushed the boat out with the decorations.'

'As care homes go, it's a pretty good one,' Nathan said. 'Charity is forever singing its praises.'

The noise of an engine ended the slightly stilted conversation, and Petra's battered but perfectly serviceable Land Rover trundled into view. It was towing a horse trailer, and Nathan watched Amos expertly manoeuvre it into position.

As soon as it came to a halt, Nathan opened up the back of it and lowered the ramp. 'You can bring Gerald out, if you want,' he said to Megan. 'Have you loaded anything into a horsebox before?'

'This is a first for me,' she said.

'He'll load okay. He's as good as gold.' The donkey was a sweet old thing, and was utterly placid – Petra wouldn't risk taking him to the care home if he wasn't bombproof.

However, Nathan wasn't about to let Megan do this by herself, although he did try to stand back and only offer advice when it was needed, until the donkey was eventually settled into the trailer, and he and Megan were free to climb aboard the Land Rover.

'Come, Patch,' he called, and the dog leapt into the footwell, where he turned in a circle and curled up in a ball.

Although this wasn't the first time Nathan had seen Amos in his Father Christmas glory, he couldn't help laughing out loud. The man was the epitome of Santa Claus, although maybe not quite as rotund as was traditional. His crinkly eyes peered at Nathan from above a surprisingly realistic beard, and Amos was also sporting some white bushy eyebrows.

'Are those caterpillars above your eyes?' Nathan chortled. 'Or did you raid Petra's stash of cotton wool?'

'Cheeky beggar, these are my own. I've sprayed them with some white stuff to make them look more authentic.'

'Have you thought about trimming them?' Nathan was trying to hold back his laughter and failing dismally.

'Let me see?' Megan said from the backseat, and Amos turned around and waggled them at her. 'Oh, my,' she said, flinching. 'They are rather full.'

'Full? They could have a postcode all of their own.' Nathan slapped his thigh, his laughter ringing out.

Amos said, 'As for you, you grumpy git, I didn't think you had a laugh in you.' He glared at Nathan, but Nathan could tell he didn't mean it. Amos gave him a final stare, then turned the volume on the radio up to drown out Nathan's chuckles.

For some reason, Nathan was feeling lighthearted and almost (not quite) in a festive frame of mind, and this feeling was heightened when they pulled up outside the care home and he saw the lights festooning the outside.

It was a two-storey, sprawling building, shaped along three sides of a square, with the open side featuring a courtyard, well-maintained gardens and glorious views of the surrounding hillsides. The open side was hidden from the front of the building and the car park, and this was where they were headed, Nathan discovered, when Charity, bundled up against the cold in a padded coat with a fur hood, dashed across the tarmac to meet them.

'We thought you could come in through the French doors via the garden, rather than simply appear in reception.'

Nathan caught the question on Megan's face and he explained that the cafe was more of a meeting place between the two wings of the home, where visitors and residents alike could help themselves to drinks and a variety of cakes and snacks. 'It serves as the focal point of the care home,' he said. 'It's almost like being in a real cafe, but you don't have to pay.'

'I'll unlock the side gate for you,' Charity said, 'and the panniers are over there, along with a couple of sacks of presents. They're all labelled,' she told Amos, 'But when you call the names out you may have to shout, although there are plenty of staff on hand for those who can't hear so well, or aren't as able to join in.'

The donkey walked down the ramp without any fuss as soon as the horsebox was opened, his ears swivelling from side to side as he took in his surroundings. He didn't object when the unfamiliar panniers were put on his back, although he did bray loudly once, just in case there happened to be any other donkeys nearby.

Plodding behind Nathan and Megan as they led him through the gate, Gerald seemed perfectly happy, especially when Nathan produced half an apple from his pocket and fed it to him. Patch walked obediently at heel, and stayed close to his master.

The sound of **Away in a Manger** being sung by a multitude of quavering voices (and one or two more strident ones) reached them as they rounded the corner, and when Nathan saw the large tree in the centre of the garden gleaming with fairy lights, and the row of expectant faces through the window, he was glad Charity had thought of the idea.

'It must be hard being in a care home at this time of year,' he murmured in Megan's ear, as Amos strode forward, a huge smile on his face and crying, 'Ho, ho, ho.'

Megan whispered back, 'I'm so glad you're doing this – look at their faces.'

Nathan scanned the lined faces of the residents, and his heart sang. Bless them, they looked so hopeful and excited, like children, and they all wore smiles. One old lady was banging her fists on her wheelchair in excitement, and another kept trying to get out of her seat but was gently held back by one of the staff. It was best if everyone stayed seated whilst the donkey was on the premises, Nathan thought; he didn't want to risk any delicate toes being trodden on, or Gerald tossing his rather hard head and bumping into someone.

As Amos cheerily handed out the presents from the panniers, Nathan kept his attention on the donkey – most of the time, because he kept having to drag his gaze away from Megan, who was helping the residents open their presents (some people wanted to save theirs for the morning) and chatting away to them. And everywhere she went, Patch was right there with her.

She knelt next to chairs and patted gnarled hands. She smiled and kissed wrinkled cheeks, and had a word to say to everyone. He noticed how good she was with them, how patient and kind, and how she offered to bring them cups of tea, glasses of eggnog or sherry, or mince pies, and how they responded to her. And even though he could guess how hard this time of year must be for her, her smile appeared more open, and she seemed freer and less uptight as the evening wore on. So maybe this was doing her as much good as it was the elderly people she was spending time with?

'I want you to sing my song,' Amos declared, once all the presents were distributed.

'What song is that?' asked William, the care home manager, with a wink.

'Why, **Jingle Bells**, of course!' Amos clutched his belly and ho, ho, ho-ed again, to gales of laughter and raised glasses.

'I'm surprised they allow alcohol,' Megan said to Nathan, coming to stand next to him and Gerald, who was half-asleep with one small hind hoof cocked and his head hanging down.

'I've been told it's one of the better care homes,' Nathan said. 'Not only is there this cafe, but they serve three courses at lunch and dinner, and wine if anyone wants it. There's a gym, a spa and a hairdresser, a library and a games room. And there's a full list of activities every day.'

'Crumbs, it's like a hotel!' she said, putting her mouth next to his ear as she tried to make herself heard over the enthusiastic warbling and the plinking of piano keys.

'It's not cheap,' he replied. 'But it's worth the money if you can afford it; they do take great care of their residents.'

'I can see that. Thank you for letting me come with you. I've enjoyed myself.'

So had Nathan. It made a pleasant change from lolling in front of the telly and feeling slightly sorry for himself, which was what he usually did on Christmas Eve. Christmas was just a bit too in your face, he thought. It could often highlight what you hadn't got as much as what you had; and he hadn't got anyone apart from Patch. And the stables. But then, he wasn't a member of the family as such. He couldn't forget he was an employee, for all that Petra and Amos went out of their way to make him feel included, valued and liked.

He supposed he could have taken some holiday leave and spent a few days with his mum or his siblings. But as much as he loved them, he always got itchy feet after a couple of hours and was glad to go back home. He'd never manage a whole day, and certainly not three or four. No, he was better off staying put, and enjoying his lunch tomorrow at the stables – after he'd helped turn the horses out into the fields and muck out, that is!

Nathan's social battery was running low by the time he loaded Gerald back into the horsebox. There was only so much socialising he could tolerate, and he was grateful for Megan coming along to take some of the attention off him. He'd not smiled as much in ages, and his cheeks ached as a result. He hadn't made a fool of himself and neither had he been too grumpy he thought, pleased with how well the evening had gone. Gerald had behaved himself impeccably, and so had Patch, who'd been a great hit with those folks who liked dogs. Amos had brought good cheer (and presents), but the star of the show, Nathan felt, had been Megan. The residents had loved her, and when she'd waved goodbye her ears must have rung with all the pleadings for her to come back and visit them soon.

She'd promised she would, and Nathan believed her. He didn't think she was the type to make a promise if she didn't intend to keep it.

After they'd put a bemused Gerald back in his stable and closed the door, Amos yawned hugely and invited them in for a nightcap before they went home, then wandered into the house, leaving Nathan and Megan alone.

Nathan glanced across the yard, golden light from the windows spilling out onto the old cobbles. He could see Amos enter the kitchen, and Petra turn to speak to him.

'I'd best be getting off,' he decided, calling Patch to heel. The terrier had been rooting around in the straw of the donkey's stall, but as soon as he heard his name, he leapt up at the half-door and scrabbled over the top of it to drop down to the ground.

'Well I never!' Megan exclaimed. 'If I hadn't seen him do that with my own eyes, I wouldn't have believed it.' She bent to pet him. 'You are so bouncy for a little dog,' she crooned. 'Yes, you are.'

Patch lapped up the attention, leaning against her leg in bliss as she ruffled his ears.

'You were marvellous with the old people,' Nathan said.

'I enjoyed talking to them,' Megan replied. 'And I think they had a good time. As did I.'

'Me too.' He stared at her awkwardly, wondering what to say next. 'Um, Merry Christmas.' He cringed, guessing that was probably not the most sensitive thing to say to her under the circumstances.

'You, too.' She hesitated, then stepped towards him, and to his dismay and delight her arms came around him and she pulled him into a hug.

Oh, my, it felt amazing to be held by her, however briefly, and he inhaled her perfume and closed his eyes for a second, relishing the feel of her as he hugged her back.

Without meaning to, and certainly without any conscious thought, Nathan kissed her on the cheek. His lips encountered soft skin and it was all he could do not to kiss her again, but this time it wouldn't be on her cheek. He wanted to taste her lips, to feel the heat of her mouth—

Bugger.

His heart was racing so fast he thought he might pass out, and he hastily released her and backed away.

'Er, see you after Christmas,' he said, not daring to look at her for fear of what he might see. She was probably as appalled as he. What had possessed him to do such a thing? He was the least touchy-feely person he knew. He'd never been a hugger, and for him to have hugged her back so enthusiastically had shocked him. And then he'd **kissed** her...

He remained motionless as she wished him Merry Christmas again and walked towards her car. He stayed where he was as she got in and started the engine, flashing her headlights at him as she reversed, and then drove off.

He was still standing there five minutes later, long after her taillights had disappeared.

Nathan felt like giving himself a stern talking to, but it was impossible while his lips tingled and his heart throbbed, and an unexpected elation made his pulse race and his stomach turn over. And all he was able to do was to ask himself how come he could feel happy and glum at the same time.

Megan didn't expect to enjoy Christmas in the slightest, but when she woke on Christmas morning to see a fine blanket of snow on the ground, her spirits lifted. However, it wasn't long before they plummeted again as she contemplated the fact that she wouldn't be able to go riding in it. Only for them to lift again, because it meant she still had two more riding lessons to look forward to. Anyway, the white stuff didn't hang around for long and by the time she arrived at her parents' house it had all but gone.

It didn't stop her wondering how the horses were faring, though. Had they been let out to play in it, or were they going to spend the day in their nice warm stables? And how was Gerald feeling after his visit to the care home last night? She must remember to take him a little treat next time.

Thinking of the animals inevitably led her to thinking about Nathan. He'd seemed out of his comfort zone yesterday and she could tell he didn't enjoy being around so many people, but hats off to him for going regardless. She had to admire him for that.

Oh, who was she kidding? He hadn't **just** popped into her head – she'd been thinking about him all night. He'd lodged himself in her mind as soon as his arms had reluctantly gone around her as she'd impulsively hugged him, and she'd felt his solid body against hers, and felt the strength of his embrace, and smelt his outdoorsy scent that was a mixture of washing powder, shower gel, and the almost imperceptible aroma of horse and leather. It was intoxicating and she'd breathed him in, letting the scent of him wash over her and through her.

And then he'd kissed her.

Okay, so it was a maiden aunt kiss on the cheek and he'd certainly not meant anything by it, but the brief feel of his warm lips on her skin had shocked her. In a nice way.

Or maybe not. She hadn't been at all prepared for the way she'd reacted, and it had left her out of sorts for the rest of the night. And today, too.

What shocked her the most was the way she'd wanted to turn her head and feel his mouth on hers. She'd wanted him to kiss her properly, the way lovers kiss. And the knowledge had both appalled and excited her.

That he didn't feel anything for her had been evidenced by his awkwardness when they were saying goodbye.

Without warning, a longing to see him engulfed her, and she simply didn't know how she was going to get through the next few days of forced Christmas jollity, and the pity and concern of her parents.

Nathan wasn't a whistler. He disliked whistling and never did it. So why was he whistling now? He'd caught himself, lips puckered and a toneless high-pitched noise emanating from his mouth, and he'd immediately stopped making such a dreadful racket. Even Patch was looking askance at him, and Hercules had given him a thoroughly disgusted glare when he'd gone to take him to the field.

Thankfully, only the animals had heard him, so there was no one to ask him why he was so chirpy. Because if someone had, he wouldn't have a clue what to say to them.

And he didn't have a clue what to say to himself. There was no reason for him to feel cheerful. No reason at all.

Maybe if Megan had reacted in a positive way to the kiss he'd given her, he might have a reason; but she hadn't. In fact, their goodbye had been embarrassing and awkward, and he'd be surprised if she didn't go out of her way to avoid him in future.

So there was absolutely no reason at all for him to be so jaunty.

Reining himself in, he finished all the jobs he'd set himself, then went to the farmhouse to wash his hands and change out of his work clothes. He'd brought a clean pair of jeans with him and a checked flannel shirt, and in no time at all he was looking presentable. He probably could have done with a shave, but a bit of stubble helped keep his face warm this time of year. His hair could do with a trim, too. And was that a new wrinkle running down the side of his nose to his mouth? He had another one on the other side, he noticed, peering into the speckled mirror of the downstairs loo and shower room.

Meh, so what? He was getting older, and he should expect his face to show his age.

Megan looked younger than hers though, he mused. She was forty-three but he remembered when he'd first set eyes on her that he'd estimated her to be anywhere between thirty and forty.

He wondered what she was doing now. Was she thinking about him?

No, of course she wasn't. Stop being so daft, he told himself. He'd kissed her on the cheek, in the same way she'd kissed many of Honeymead's residents last night. It had meant nothing to her.

But it had meant something to him, and he still wasn't sure what had possessed him to do it.

He couldn't stop thinking about it,
though: he couldn't stop thinking about
her. The way her arms had snaked around
him, the way she'd felt so delicate, yet so
soft and yielding. Her perfume, the
smoothness of her skin, her luminous
eyes.

'Are you okay in there?' Amos yelled
outside the bathroom door.

'Eh? Er, yeah, I'll be out now,' he called,
then muttered, 'Pull yourself together,
man,' and grimaced. His reflection
snarled back at him. That's more like it,
he thought. All that smiling didn't sit well
on his face.

Thankful he'd got his wayward emotions
under control, he settled down to enjoy
the sumptuous lunch which Amos, Petra
and Harry had prepared between them.
Roast turkey with all the trimmings,
pumpkin soup to start, and Christmas pud
with brandy sauce for afters, it was a
feast for a king, and by the time Nathan

forced the last spoonful of pudding into his mouth, he was so full he thought he might pop.

Everyone else at the table had also made a good fist of their lunch, but there were loads left in the tureens, which Amos began to decant into a huge pan ready for the traditional Boxing Day meal of bubble and squeak.

Petra groaned. 'I'm stuffed.' She made to get up.

Nathan put out his hand. 'Stay where you are, all of you. I'll clear away and stack the dishwasher. It's the least I can do – that was stunning. I don't think I'll eat for a week.'

'I take it there's no point in me wrapping up some turkey for you to have for supper?' Amos teased.

'Go on, then. I might be able to manage a bite or two later.'

As he was dealing with the saucepans, Nathan caught himself mid-pucker and realised he was about to whistle again, so as a distraction he stuck his head into the living room to ask if anyone wanted a cuppa. They'd shared a bottle of wine during lunch, and Amos had treated himself to a small sherry beforehand, but Nathan guessed a cup of tea would go down better than alcohol considering the horses would have to be brought in later.

He almost barked out a laugh at the sight of Amos and Petra fast asleep, Amos with his mouth open, Petra with her head on Harry's shoulder. All three were still wearing the party hats that had come out of the crackers, and they looked so comical Nathan chuckled. Petra's had slipped down over her ears and the paper hat covered most of her face; Amos's was balanced on the top of his head, and the cat was trying to bat it with a paw.

Nathan left them to it and finished tidying up, and when he was done he whispered goodbye to Harry, who was watching The Wizard of Oz through half-closed eyes.

Despite having enjoyed himself, Nathan was relieved to return to his own house, and he plodded down the lane in the encroaching darkness, his faithful dog at his heels and a foil-wrapped packet of turkey in his pocket. He'd spent enough time with people over the past day or so, and he desperately needed some solitude.

Yet when he opened the door to his cottage and stepped inside, the silence hit him like walking into a wall. There wasn't a sound; not even a creak or groan from the pipes, and without warning he was overcome by a feeling of loneliness.

Is this how it is for Megan, he wondered? He couldn't imagine feeling like this all the time, and he shuddered. It was rare for him to feel lonely, but he guessed that for Megan it was commonplace. Pity gripped him, and he wished he could do something to help her.

She was right not to get a dog, but maybe a cat would help? At least it would be someone to come home to after a hard day in the office he mused, clutching Patch to him and giving him a cuddle, grateful for the warm little body snuggling into him.

She was probably right to think about changing jobs too, and an image of her expression as she waited for the verdict on the cake she'd made swam into his mind. It sounded as though she only had her job in HR in her life, and if she didn't enjoy it, then she needed to seriously think about changing careers.

He knew it was easier said than done, but he couldn't think of anything worse than spending eight or more hours a day in a job he disliked. It must be soul-destroying.

Thankfully he loved his, and as he'd said to Megan, it might not make him rich but as long as he had enough money to live on he didn't need any more. Although Petra was his boss, she let him get on with stuff, and if there was anything to be done, she wrote it on the whiteboard in the office and he ticked the job off when he'd completed it – it was as good as being his own boss but without the headache.

But almost without his noticing, loneliness stole over him again and he began to wonder if, like Megan, his life was also missing something.

Nathan tried to ignore the odd and unsettling feeling, but it kept invading his thoughts throughout the rest of the evening, and although he tried, he couldn't shift it, especially when Megan slipped into his mind once more.

CHAPTER SEVEN

'Over here,' Nathan called as Megan got out of her car and headed towards the arena, and she stopped and turned at the sound of his voice. It made her heart lurch, but she tried not to let it show. He didn't need to know she was starting to get a bit of a crush on him.

'Did you have a good Christmas?' she asked, walking towards him. He was saddling Hercules, and Sherbet was patiently standing next to the stallion, her saddle already on her back.

'Yes, thanks. You?'

She pulled a face. 'It was okay, considering...' She let the rest of the sentence hang, knowing he'd get what she meant.

'I'm sorry,' he said.

'For what?' The brief brush of his lips on her cheek? She hadn't been able to stop thinking about it all over the festive season.

'For your husband passing on. You must miss him.'

Megan blinked at the unexpected comment. 'Yes, I do,' she replied honestly.

Nathan studied her, then he nodded slowly before turning back to his task, leaving her to wonder what all that was about.

'Are you taking me out today? I assume we're going on a hack,' she asked.

'Is that okay?'

'You or the hack?'

'Either? Both?'

'I want to ride out onto the hills today, and I'm perfectly happy that it's you who will be accompanying me.'

'I thought we'd take the same route we'll be taking when it snows,' he said, and Megan felt a momentary pang. This was her penultimate ride. The next one was weather dependent, and when that was done, her visits to the stables would be over.

Unless...?

She could always make hacking a regular feature. Her rediscovered love of riding didn't have to end on the next snowfall. There was nothing stopping her from booking herself in for more rides.

Or was there?

She glanced across at Nathan, who was sitting astride Hercules and adjusting the stirrup length. More rides meant she'd see more of Nathan, possibly on a regular basis, and she didn't intend to put herself in a position where she might fall for a man who didn't think of her in that way.

On that basis, it was probably better to knock the horse-riding on the head as soon as Jeremy's final gift was completed.

His final gift...

She felt incredibly sad to think there wouldn't be any more envelopes with her name on and his handwritten card inside. It was as though he was severing his last link with her, as though he was pushing her away. Which was ridiculous, but she couldn't help how she felt or the thoughts that flitted through her mind.

Megan mounted up and without being asked Sherbet fell into line behind

Hercules, leaving Megan free to dwell on the implications of no longer having this last link with Jeremy. It was both frightening and liberating, and she wasn't sure how to deal with it.

Sherbet breaking into a trot pulled Megan out of herself and forced her to pay attention to the here and now or risk an injury. A rising trot could do that to a person, as a loss of concentration could mean a hearty smack on the backside as one's behind slapped onto the saddle. Not only was it uncomfortable (probably for the horse as well as the rider), but she'd also feel more amateurish than she already felt. It didn't matter that Nathan was ahead of her and wouldn't see her incompetent horsemanship – she'd know, and that was enough.

When they reached the gate leading to the path onto the hillside above the stables, Nathan edged Hercules to the side so he could open it and Sherbet walked through, swishing her tail provocatively at the other horse and crabbing to the side.

'We'll have none of those shenanigans,' Megan told the mare firmly, catching Nathan's eye and pouting her displeasure at him.

'Is she playing you up?'

'Just being a bit flirty. Sherbet, not me.' Maybe the pout hadn't been the best facial expression to use. She didn't want him to think she was being coquettish.

'I didn't think otherwise,' he said.

That told her! If she had been flirting it would have gone over his head anyway, which reinforced her view that he wouldn't look at her twice.

And who could blame him? She was damaged goods. Not the having been married part, but the grief part. Who'd want a widow who had yet to move on from the premature death of the only man she would ever love.

Oh, and yes, that "only man she'd ever love" was a stumbling block, both for her and for any man who fell for her. Because although she was coming around to the idea of at some point in the dim and distant future having a relationship, she didn't for one second believe she'd love as deeply again.

'Oh, my, look at that view!' she exclaimed as the horses emerged onto an expanse of moorland. Below there was a patchwork of rolling fields, meadows, and pockets of woodland, interspersed with farms, and in the distance she could see Picklewick itself. She could make out the square turret of the Norman church, which seemed incredibly small this high up.

For January the afternoon was relatively bright, and although it was too soon to see any lengthening of the days, there were hints of the spring to come in the tiny buds on the hedgerows, and fresh green growth on either side of the rugged track. The air was incredibly fresh and sharp, its chill almost painful on her skin and in her lungs, but she breathed deeply, letting nature flow through her and chase away any dismal thoughts.

Nathan drew Hercules to a halt and twisted slightly in his saddle. 'Have you not been up here before?' he asked.

'Yes, but not for many years,' she replied. 'Jeremy and I always kept meaning to bring a picnic up here, but we never got round to it. I'd forgotten how lovely it is.'

Dragging her eyes away from the view, she gazed around at the golden grass, all its goodness sucked back into the roots. It rippled in the keen wind, and she stared at it mesmerised, until her attention was drawn to the rowan trees with their bright red berries poking through the russet bracken. A blackbird was perched on the uppermost branches of the nearest stubby tree, picking the berries off one by one and gulping them down. Sheep dotted the hillside, little white blobs busily searching for any grass worth eating, and high above a red kite circled, with its unmistakable forked tail and high-pitched cry.

She watched its flight for a moment, then her eyes tracked beyond it to the grey lowering clouds, and she shivered.

'It's definitely a cold one,' Nathan observed, blowing on his hands.

Even though Megan wore thick gloves, her hands were freezing, and she wondered how he could stand it. He was certainly made of hardier stuff than she.

'I reckon we're going to get that snow you want before too long,' he observed.

'There isn't anything forecast,' she said.

'There might not be, but the animals know. See those sheep?' He pointed to the distant hillside. 'If you watch them for long enough you'll see that they're all slowly but surely heading downhill. They'll be seeking out more sheltered places, ready to hunker down. The snow might not come today, and probably not tomorrow, but I reckon it will be here soon. The signs are there if you know what to look for,' he added.

'Can I ask you a favour?' She peered at him hopefully. 'Will you give me a call if it starts to snow; enough to go out for a ride in, I mean. I'd hate to miss a good opportunity, and my main concern is that if I leave it until it's snowing in the village, I won't be able to get to you, or it would be too dangerous to take the horses out.'

'Of course I will.'

'Can I ask another favour?'

He raised his eyebrows. 'Depends on what it is.' His tone was deadpan but a smile lingered around his mouth, and Megan couldn't help staring at it.

He had nice lips, well-shaped, and he didn't seem to have shaved for a couple of days. The stubble was coming through more grey than brown, unlike the hair on his head which was only greying at the temples. It made him look sexy.

Oh my God, is that what she thought?

That was a kind of step up from finding him attractive, or was it all the same thing? She honestly didn't know, but what she did know was that she felt a pull towards him deep in her gut, and he was in her head, too.

She put a hand up to her cheek where he'd kissed her the other day, before she realised what she was doing and let it drop again, resting it on the pommel of the saddle.

'Well?' he asked. 'What is the favour?'

'Oh yes, I...um...do you think you could take me on my last ride? I'm sure Petra has got lots of other things she can be going on with.'

'And I haven't?' He was grinning at her to show he was teasing.

'I expect you have, but I'd like you to join me.' She knew she was playing with fire, and the only one who would get burned was her, but for goodness sake this was only a hack, nothing more. It would be just as magical if Petra were to accompany her, but for some reason she wanted it to be Nathan.

She almost snorted at herself. **For some reason** indeed! There wasn't any "some" about it; she knew exactly what the reason was, she fancied him and she wanted to spend a bit of time with him.

But so what? She wasn't hurting anyone, and there was nothing wrong with indulging in a little bit of fantasy even though she had absolutely no intention of making any moves to fulfil it. This was just a part of the healing process. She was starting to come alive again, just like nature around her. She'd gone through a long, dark, emotional winter, and now she felt the first stirrings of her own spring in her heart and in her soul.

Megan was under no illusion that this gradual return to life she was about to embark on would be plain sailing, and just like those new shoots that were trying their best to poke through the frozen soil, she'd have her setbacks. Those shoots might soon have a covering of snow, and no doubt she'd have her own internal snowfalls to deal with along the way. But snow melted, and she realised the chill which had engulfed her heart since Jeremy left her, would also thaw.

'We'd better get a move on,' Nathan said, interrupting her thoughts. 'We've got some way to go yet.'

'Where are we heading?'

'There's an old derelict farmhouse about four miles in that direction. I thought next time I'd bring a flask, and we can stop and have a hot drink before we turn around and come back down again.'

'That's a lovely idea. I'll bring a slice of cake. I've got my first class this evening, so no doubt I'll have more cake than I'll know what to do with.'

'Good luck,' he said. 'Although I'm sure you won't need it. As for cake, we'll eat all the left-over cake you can send our way. Timothy said the one you did for him was absolutely delicious. Mind you, he only managed to have a small slice, because Charity's family dived in before he had a chance. It went down a storm, he said.'

Megan smiled. Timothy had sent her an email to thank her and had informed her that the cake had been very well received, but it hadn't lasted long, and he'd thought Charity's father might have polished off three slices all by himself. She was delighted with the compliment, and it had been a great boost to her self-esteem.

She was looking forward to this evening, and she couldn't wait to get started. She kept telling herself it was only a ten-week course, and the fact that she was taking it didn't mean she had to resign from her job and start up a business of her own. But deep down that's what she was secretly hoping might happen.

Telling herself it was far too early to start making those kinds of plans, she nevertheless wondered whether it might be possible to renegotiate her hours at work. Perhaps she could drop down to part-time, which would give her the best of both worlds.

'Do you really think I could make a go of cake decorating?' she asked abruptly, although Nathan probably wasn't the best person to chat to about this.

'I don't see why not,' he said. 'But I think you'll probably need to get some professional advice. I like a nice bit of cake, but I'm no expert.'

'I'm considering going part-time. What do you think?' She didn't know why she was asking him this, apart from that he seemed sensible and wouldn't pander to her, or humour her. She sensed he would tell her straight, even if it was something she didn't want to hear.

'It's a good solution. It gives you a safety net.'

'That's what I was thinking. But I won't do it just yet. I want to complete the course first, and get some more experience under my belt. I'm also going to have to come up with a business plan. I've got an awful lot to do and to think about before I take the plunge. And anyway, it's not as though I've got any other distractions in the evenings or the weekends. I can carry on working and make cakes side by side.'

'Will you carry on with the riding?'

Megan caught him looking at her out of the corner of his eye, and suddenly she had a feeling her answer was important. 'I had considered it,' she replied slowly.

She might. Then again, she might not, and she was leaning more towards the might not than the might. She was enjoying this ride and she'd most definitely enjoy the next one, but that would be the end of it. She would have indulged herself enough. This final gift of Jeremy's would have served its purpose.

As she listened to the steady plod of the horses' hooves as they climbed up the path, the old farmhouse growing gradually closer, she tried to imagine Jeremy by her side – but all she could see was Nathan, a man who was very much here, very much alive, and very much in her thoughts. And she'd never felt so conflicted or uncertain in her life.

'You go on into the house and get warm,' Nathan said, noticing how cold Megan looked as they rode into the yard. 'I'll see to the horses.' Déjà vu, but this time instead of insisting on helping him, she handed him Sherbet's reins, gave him a small smile, and went inside.

Her car was still in the car park by the time he was done, so he didn't linger after he'd finished for the day. Instead, he collected Patch who had sensibly been snuggling in the warm, and headed off home, his thoughts consumed by her.

Cross with himself for letting anyone upset his composure, he clattered around in his kitchen preparing a hot meal, and ate it in sullen silence.

He'd known it would have been better not to have taken Megan out for a trek, but Petra was looking so peaky he hadn't had the heart to refuse her.

Never mind, he told himself, only one more ride to go, and that would be the end of it.

A part of him (a bigger part than he was prepared to admit) was sorry, and he felt a strange ache in his chest at the thought of never seeing Megan again, but it was for the best. She wasn't ready, and when the time came for her to move on with her life, he was not the man she'd choose. He knew that. What could he offer her? He was a solitary, grumpy, middle-aged fellow, who barely had a penny to his name and spent most of his time repairing fences, shovelling manure or driving a tractor.

Clearly, Megan was used to far better than the likes of him.

But however much he tried to turn his thoughts away from her, she invaded his mind, and Nathan had a niggling feeling she was invading his heart, too.

'That's it, we're done,' Megan said, putting her mug on the table and getting to her feet.

Petra felt relief wash over her. She hadn't been looking forward to hashing out the details of creating and placing an advert, but when Megan had stayed on at the stables after her ride in order to help with the recruitment process, she'd been a godsend. Okay, she'd asked questions Petra hadn't known how to answer (holiday entitlement being one of them –

and she still had to speak to Nathan about his, because the man rarely took a day off), but with Megan's calm and sure guidance, the advert was finally done and posted online. She'd also printed it out so Petra could ask shops in the village if they'd display a copy for her.

Hopefully, there would be some interest; after all, Picklewick was in a rural area where agricultural and farm jobs were commonplace, so there was a talent pool available. And although she hadn't said as much to Megan, Petra was only interested in whether applicants had an affinity with horses and whether she felt she could get on with them. Petra also made a note to have Nathan sit in on the interviews – he had to get on with the new person too, because he'd be working quite closely with him or her.

Petra blew out her cheeks and got to her feet. 'Thanks for that,' she said. 'Let me pay you.'

'Don't be daft! It's a pleasure.' Megan waved her hand.

'How about a couple of rides, instead? After your snow one? Maybe a few in the spring when the weather breaks?'

'I don't know…'

'Haven't you enjoyed your rides?' Petra frowned. She could have sworn Megan had thoroughly enjoyed herself. Had something happened to make her change her mind?

'I've enjoyed them very much. It's just…' Megan sighed. 'I understand why Jeremy bought them for me and I truly appreciate it and the sentiment behind it, but…' She sighed again. 'I'm not sure I'm ready to put myself out there again.'

Petra was thoroughly baffled. 'It's a couple of rides, not a marriage proposal,' she began, then she stopped and her eyes widened. 'Is it Nathan?'

'Not at all.'

Petra noted the twin spots of colour on Megan's cheeks. **That's the way the land lies, is it,** she mused, never expecting that the still-grieving woman who had arrived at the stables a little over a month ago was beginning to have feelings for Nathan. And Petra wondered what Nathan felt about that – or whether he actually knew. Knowing him, he was probably oblivious.

'It's not like that,' Megan insisted.

'Like what?' Petra asked, innocently.

Megan took a deep breath and drew herself up. 'Thank you for the offer, but I don't think I'll be doing any more riding. It's been lovely, but I can't see a future in it.'

As Petra thanked Megan again for her help and showed her out, she reflected that "see a future" was an odd thing to say in response to the offer of a couple of hacks, and Petra got the distinct impression Megan was referring to something else entirely – something to do with Nathan.

Petra vowed to take a closer look at what was going on between the two of them: she loved Nathan like a brother and she wanted him to be happy, and from what she'd seen of Megan, the woman was ready to embrace life and love again.

Petra, smiling wickedly, had never considered herself to be a matchmaker, but if there was any possibility these two might find love together, she'd do her utmost to make it happen.

'Hi, Megan, it's Petra.' Megan automatically glanced out of her living room window, but she knew Petra wasn't phoning because it was snowing and there was a hack to go on. It was dark outside, for one thing, and for another it was gone eight o'clock in the evening.

'Is everything okay?' A trickle of worry entered her mind.

'It's Nathan—'

The trickle turned into a torrent. 'Oh god, is he all right? Has he had an accident?' Horses could be dangerous, everyone knew that. They had hooves and teeth, and were so large and heavy—

'If you'd let me finish, I was just about to say that it's Nathan's birthday on Saturday, and I was hoping you'd make a cake for him. We're having a little do in the Black Horse.'

Relief made Megan weak and she sagged back in her armchair.

'Yes,' she managed to get out, ashamed of her outburst. 'When do you want me to bring it to the stables? Saturday morning?'

'I was thinking you could bring it with you when you come to the pub.'

'What pub?'

'The Black Horse – keep up.' Petra huffed down the phone.

'You want **me** to go to the Black Horse?'

'You'll have to if you want to help Nathan celebrate his birthday. Either way, it seems pointless you driving all the way up to the stables with the cake, only for me to drive it all the way back to Picklewick again. Are you coming, or not? There'll be a buffet, and I'll even buy you your first drink. What do you say?'

'I'm surprised Nathan has agreed to a party – he doesn't seem the party type.'

'He is when you get to know him,' Petra replied breezily. 'Look, I've got to go. I'll leave the design up to you. He likes a nice Victoria sponge with raspberry jam.'

'Thanks for the—'

Too late, Petra had hung up, leaving Megan bewildered. One moment she'd been scared out of her wits at the thought of Nathan being thrown or trampled, and the next she was being advised of his cake preferences.

So much for her decision to have nothing more to do with the stables once she'd ridden her last hack.

However, she hadn't done that yet, so technically she wasn't going back on her decision. Plus it would be another opportunity to get one of her cakes in front of more eyes than just her fellow students on the course. And she didn't want Nathan to think she'd been invited and had refused. He didn't deserve to be snubbed like that. Another plus would be that the cake could be her present to him, and she wouldn't have to figure out what he might like. Buying for men was always tricky, and she used to struggle with ideas of what to get Jeremy for Christmas and birthdays.

She'd do it, she decided. She could pop into the pub with the cake, stay for a drink, then head off home. Once she'd shown her face she would have done her duty and no one would miss her if she sloped off early.

Her excitement for Saturday made its presence known in the clenching of her tummy and she frowned at herself before she realised she was bound to be excited – this was a great opportunity to showcase what she could do in terms of cake creation.

And she had the perfect cake in mind!

'Saturday, you said?' Nathan shot Amos a look out of the corner of his eye as he stretched the hen's wing out to check her feathers. She'd been off-colour lately and Nathan wondered if she was being picked on by the other birds. 'I haven't played darts for years. There must be someone else you can call on?'

'Can't think of anyone. We've asked all those who are any good.'

'Thanks a lot!'

'You know what I mean. We just need you to make up the numbers. It's the semi-final.'

'Why can't Scouse play?'

'He's had to go to Liverpool. Family emergency. I told you that.'

'So you did.' But Nathan had a feeling something was up, and he didn't know what. Amos's story didn't ring true. He put the bird on the ground, and it dashed off with an indignant squawk. 'Hen-pecked,' he said.

'Scouse? **Is he?** Crumbs!' Amos shook his head in disbelief.

'The **hen**.'

'Oh, I see. What about it, then? Are you up for it, only they won't let us play if we're a man short.'

'Have you asked any of the women? Or does it have to be a man?' Nathan was only teasing, but Amos looked shifty all of a sudden.

'You're our last hope,' Amos insisted. 'I'll treat you to supper and a pint.'

'Make it two pints,' Nathan said.

'Done!' Amos held out his hand and the two men shook on it.

'Just one thing – I thought darts were always on a Friday?'

'Er, yeah, but not this week.'

Nathan sighed. He didn't particularly like darts, but he supposed it would give him something to do on Saturday night, other than sit at home and stare at the telly. It was his birthday, too, so it would be nice to get out even if no one remembered.

Ah, that was it!

Amos **had** remembered, which was why he was so insistent Nathan went to the Black Horse on Saturday. Knowing how Nathan hated a fuss, Amos had come up with the story that he was needed for the darts match in order to buy him a pub meal and a couple of pints.

If that was the worst Amos would do (aside from Petra buying him a card and a bottle of something malty and mellow), Nathan could deal with that.

In fact, he was looking forward to it.

Megan was thrilled with the cake she'd made for Nathan, even if she did say so herself, and she hoped he'd be as pleased.

She'd toyed with a horsey theme because of his connection to the stables, but in the end had gone with her instinct that he'd appreciate a Patch cake instead. Which was why she was walking up to the door of the Black Horse and carrying a box, inside of which was a cake in the shape of a Jack Russell terrier, complete with a dark brown patch over the dog's eye. It looked the spitting image of Nathan's furry friend.

She was concentrating so hard on not dropping it and trying to hold an umbrella aloft which was wedged between her elbow and her body (the snow had yet to materialise, although what was falling from the sky this evening was more sleet than rain) that she nearly walked into a person who was also hurrying towards the door.

'Oops, sorry,' she said, almost poking the man in the head with her umbrella.

He pushed the hood of his parker back and her eyes widened as Nathan stepped in front of her and opened the door. 'After you.'

Megan slipped into the porch, grateful to get out of the dreadful weather and Patch trotted in behind her. Not knowing whether the cake was to be a surprise to be brought out at the end of the evening, her smile was more of a grimace, and she hoped she hadn't been rumbled.

'I'll just, erm...' she said, nodding towards the door to the main bar and hoping she'd spot Petra.

'Is that a cake?'

'Erm, yes. Someone ordered it. I'm meeting them here.'

'Can I buy you a drink?'

'Shouldn't I be buying you one? Happy birthday, by the way,' she added as he also opened this door for her.

'How do you know it's my—'

'Surprise!' a chorus of voices yelled and Megan jumped, almost dropping the cake box.

Nathan looked stunned. And not particularly happy.

Megan saw Petra sitting at a table with Harry, Amos, Timothy and a load of other people, and she shot across the room. 'Here's the cake,' she cried, thrusting it at Petra.

Petra took hold of it and passed it straight to Harry before leaping to her feet and darting to the door. Megan turned in time to see Nathan hastening out of it.

'He hates fuss,' Amos said to her. 'I had to get him here under false pretences.'

'He didn't know about the party?'

'He wouldn't have come if he had. Leave Petra to sort him out, take off your coat and have a drink. What's your poison?'

'A white wine, please. But I won't stay long.'

'You'll stay for the buffet, won't you? Dave, the landlord, has put on a lovely spread in the back room.'

'Um, okay. I can manage a sandwich.'

Harry said, 'I'll just take this out the back, then I'll go to the bar.'

Megan shuffled out of her coat and draped it over the back of a vacant chair, before sitting down. Oh dear, this wasn't going so well, was it? The birthday boy didn't appear to appreciate his surprise party and had done a runner, and she worried he might lay an equal amount of blame on her shoulders for being party to the deception.

Eventually, though, Nathan came back in with Petra (she had a firm grip on his hand and was towing him behind her) and he was persuaded to take a seat and drink the pint put in front of him.

Megan sipped her wine and gradually relaxed. She knew everyone at their table, and although many people came up to wish an embarrassed Nathan a happy birthday, she didn't feel out of place.

That Nathan was sitting next to her and kept giving her reassuring glances, went some way to her growing enjoyment of the evening.

Nathan was well-liked and, although he was shy, by the time he'd finished his third pint, she could tell he was beginning to mellow and might even be enjoying himself.

Telling herself she was going to leave as soon as the cake was unveiled (or unboxed, as the case may be), Megan accepted another glass of wine, and vowed to do her best to enjoy the occasion; this was the first time she'd been to a party since Jeremy died, and she knew that if she was to fully immerse herself in her life there would be many more firsts to come.

But after the buffet had been well and truly tucked into, and the cake had been presented to a scowling Nathan and Happy Birthday had been sung, Megan was still rooted firmly in her chair. She was having a thoroughly lovely time, and when another glass of wine was placed in front of her, she settled back in her seat.

As she did so, Nathan's foot brushed against hers and she automatically moved hers away, only for it to happen again.

And a third time.

Oh, goodness, was he playing footsie?

A surge of desire swept over her, and she inhaled sharply at the unfamiliar feeling. Gosh, the wine was going to her head.

She caught his eye and smiled hesitantly, relieved when he grinned back at her. His foot found hers again and this time, instead of moving her own away, she slipped it out of her shoe and ran her toes along what she hoped was the top of his foot.

His expression didn't change, but hers did as she realised that unless Nathan possessed incredibly hairy feet it wasn't Nathan's foot she was stroking...

Stricken, she bent down and looked under the table.

Patch stared lovingly back at her.

Megan straightened up, her cheeks flooding with colour. 'I'm just going to step outside for a moment,' she said to no one in particular, then fanned her face with her hands to indicate she was hot.

Hurriedly, she got up from the table and fled out of the bar, feeling certain that flames of mortification must be trailing along in her wake. She hadn't been telling fibs – she honestly did feel hot. And silly.

As soon as she stepped outside, the freezing air hit her and she took a deep lungful of it. At least the sleet had stopped so she wouldn't have to go back in looking like a drowned rat. Maybe she could wait here until someone went in, and she could ask them to fetch her coat for her, to save her having to go back inside.

Feeling like an idiot, she slumped against the wall, her breath misting around her head and waited.

No one went in.

But someone did come out, and it was the very person she was hoping not to see.

'Nathan,' she said, in resignation. It would have to be him, wouldn't it?

'Are you okay? I saw you leave in a hurry.'

'I'm fine, just a bit hot.'

'I noticed Patch was cosying up to you. He's like a hot water bottle.' He joined her in leaning against the wall.

'Yes, that must have been it,' she said, feeling the chill of the bricks on her back.

'Thank you for coming.'

'You're welcome. I didn't know it was a surprise, though. You didn't seem too pleased.'

'I don't do parties, especially when I'm the guest of honour.'

'Sorry.'

'What for?'

'I wouldn't have made you a cake if I'd known you wouldn't like your party.'

'I like my cake. It's a wonderful cake and it looks just like Patch.' Nathan pushed himself up off the wall and turned to face her. 'Thank you. You knew exactly what I'd like.'

Megan smiled.

Nathan smiled back.

Before she could register what was happening, either she moved towards him or he took a step closer to her, but whatever it was she was suddenly in his arms and his mouth was on hers, and she was kissing him.

He tasted of real ale and icing, and the stubble on his chin rasped against her skin.

It was intoxicating and terrifying, and her breath caught in her throat as she breathed in the tantalising scent of him. Her legs shaking, he deepened the kiss until he was crushing her to him, and the low moan he made in the back of his throat sent her dizzy with desire.

Then the bang of the pub door dragged her abruptly back to her senses, and with a gasp she pulled away, horrified at what she'd done.

Tears gathering in her eyes, Megan took a step back, then another, ignoring the imploring hand Nathan held out to her and the beseeching look in his eyes.

She couldn't do this. She wasn't ready.

She didn't know if she ever would be.

And with that, she fled, back to her heartache and away from the promise of a love-filled future.

CHAPTER EIGHT

'I told you it was going to snow,' Nathan said to Petra, 'and Amos agreed with me. He said he could smell it in the air.'

Large fat flakes were drifting lazily to the ground, but Nathan knew this was only the start of it. Very soon they would be turning to flurries, and they would fall thick and fast, but he had a feeling it wouldn't last long.

'It might be a good idea for you to ring Megan,' he said to his boss. They were both in the office, Petra scowling at the laptop, and Nathan rubbing one of the jobs off the whiteboard.

'Why can't you do it?' she asked.

'I think it would be better coming from you. She said she'd be able to get time off work at a moment's notice, but I bet you she doesn't even realise it's snowing up here. It's probably just drizzling lower down.'

'I still can't see why you don't ring her.'

Nathan scowled. The last thing he wanted to do was to ring Megan. Tell a lie, he **did** want to speak to Megan, he wanted to hear her voice, he wanted to see her smile, her pretty face, the way she wrinkled her nose when she was thinking... He wanted to kiss her again (and again, and again) but she'd made it very clear how she felt about him.

He understood, guessing it was too much, too soon, and she wasn't ready.

Maybe she never would be. He hoped that wasn't the case: she was too beautiful, too young and too lovely to never love again. But she'd made herself clear when she'd left the Black Horse on Saturday evening.

He'd not hurt this bad in a long time, but he'd get over it. He just had to be patient, and avoid any contact with her again, for his own peace of mind as well as for hers.

It didn't prevent him from constantly thinking about her though, and since Saturday she'd taken up permanent residence in his mind. And in his heart.

'**You** should phone her,' he insisted. 'I've got to take some silage down to the fields.'

The horses and ponies were out as usual, all of them wearing nice thick winter rugs so they wouldn't feel the cold, but if the snow began to stick they'd appreciate some extra fodder. There wasn't much nourishment in the grass at this time of year, and all the animals benefited from some supplementary feed.

'Does that mean you're not going to be able to take her out on the ride?' Petra asked.

'Doubt it. I probably won't have time.'

'Why? What else do you have to do today?'

They both looked at the whiteboard; most of the jobs had been there for a while, because they were difficult to do in the winter. They could sit there until spring, it was of no consequence, but Nathan decided now was as good time as any to have a go at fixing the baler.

He had an idea what was wrong with it and he knew it wouldn't take too long to mend, but he'd been putting it off, because while the weather had been relatively dry although cold, there was always something else that needed doing outside.

Not today though. Cold and snowing didn't entice him to work outdoors, so he might as well tackle the baler.

Petra narrowed her eyes at him. 'Okay, I'll take her out,' she agreed, and he lingered for a moment as she picked up the phone and dialled Megan's number.

'Hi Megan, it's Petra up at the stables on Muddypuddle Lane. I just thought I'd let you know it's snowing quite heavily up here so if you want to go for a ride you'd best make your way up smartish. Half an hour?' Petra looked at Nathan. 'That's fine.' There was a pause, then Petra said, 'I'll be taking you today, out if that's okay? Good, see you in a bit. All done,' Petra said to him after she ended the call. 'Can you do me a favour and bring Hercules and Sherbet in for me after you've taken the silage down?'

Nathan nodded, feeling dejected. He would have loved nothing better than to have gone riding with Megan, but he had no intention of being around when she showed up. He was doing what was right, for the right reasons. He didn't need to open himself to heartache, and he didn't need to subject her to his puppy dog eyes. She had no clue he was starting to have feelings for her, and he wanted it to stay that way.

Starting? Ha, that was a joke. It had crept up on him unannounced and ambushed him. He wasn't **starting** at all: he already had them.

It didn't take him long to load up the trailer and take it down to the fields, then he went back for the two horses and took them into the barn ready to be tacked up. After that he went in search of Petra to tell her the horses were ready for her.

He found her just coming out of the house, but she wasn't dressed for riding. She was wearing a pair of jeans, smart leather boots, and her best waxed cotton jacket.

'Where are you going?' he asked her.

'Sorry, Nathan, I've just had a phone call from the bank, and I need to pop out for a while. It can't wait, so you will have to go riding with Megan. That's okay, isn't it?'

Nathan was savvy enough to know that she wasn't asking him, she was telling him, and he had a feeling she'd planned this all along. She was up to something, but he just had to concentrate on getting through the next few hours, and by this evening Megan Barnes would be out of his life for good and he could go back to his usual insular existence.

The problem was, he had a worrying feeling he didn't **want** to go back to it!

When Petra phoned, Megan had been seriously tempted to say she couldn't get out of work, but she decided she might as well get this business over and done with. She knew she wouldn't feel right until she'd done what Jeremy wanted, which was to go horseback riding in the snow. It was his final gift to her, and she had to see it through.

After today there would be no reason for her to set foot anywhere near the stables on Muddypuddle Lane, and therefore she wouldn't see Nathan again. Hopefully she wouldn't see him today, either. She missed him though, his dry quiet ways, his steadiness, his solidity, but that was ridiculous considering she'd only known him a few weeks. The fact that she was still thinking about him was proof she needed to distance herself from him. She'd soon get over her silly infatuation and return to the way she was before.

Actually, that was quite a worrying thought. Did she honestly want to return to the miserable lacklustre person she'd been since Jeremy died?

No, she didn't.

She'd never forget her husband, of course she wouldn't – he'd always be there in her heart and her soul – but it was time to start living again.

Thankfully, Petra would be accompanying her today, so Megan should be able to stay out of Nathan's way. Her heart squeezed a little and her stomach churned, but she ignored it. She should never have kissed him, and she only had herself to blame if she was feeling rotten, but her vague guilt was more to do with how happy she'd felt in Nathan's arms and the nagging feeling that she didn't have any right to be happy. Any and all brief moments of contentment since Jeremy was gone made her feel like that, but it was lessening. She just didn't think she had been prepared for her intense reaction to Nathan's kiss, and it had taken her totally by surprise. She just hoped her erratic behaviour hadn't ruined his birthday.

Informing work she was taking the rest of the day off, she hurried home to change into her riding gear, grabbed a couple of slices of cake and made her way to the stables.

Although only two miles out of Picklewick, it was two uphill miles, and with each hundred or so foot of elevation the drizzle in the lower lying areas turned to sleet, then to soggy snowflakes which dissolved immediately upon impact, and eventually, as she pulled into the stables on Muddypuddle Lane, the snow was falling in fat thick flakes which stuck to everything they came into contact with.

It wasn't ideal weather to go riding in, and Megan hoped Petra knew what she was doing. Maybe they wouldn't go as far as the disused farmhouse. It was probably best if they didn't. The last thing

Megan wanted to do was to get lost, or stuck in a snowdrift.

When she'd gone riding in the snow as a teenager, it had been purely accidental. There had already been snow on the ground and it had lain there for a while, and as she and her friends had set off, the sky had been clear. It was a very cold, very crisp winter morning, but by the time they got halfway around the looped circuit of the mountain and were starting to head back towards the riding stables, clouds had billowed in and snow had started to fall. It had been magical, but possibly only in hindsight. When she thought back on it, Megan had remembered feeling very cold and slightly alarmed. The horses, though, knew where they were going, and just plodded, heads down, towards their nice warm stables.

Had she told Jeremy that part, the fact that she'd got soaked through and freezing, and she'd been scared about being lost?

She didn't think she had. She'd just told him how she'd turned her face up to the sky and the snowflakes had melted on her eyelashes and on her tongue, and that the world had been silent and still, and so very pretty.

Now that she was older, she thought about what could have gone wrong.

But surely Petra wouldn't have agreed to allow her to ride in the snow, if it was at all dangerous? Maybe they should wait for it to stop?

She was here now though, so she might as well carry on with it, but suggest they do a couple of laps of a field instead, rather than risk going up onto the hillside. It wouldn't be much fun anyway if she couldn't see more than a hand in front of her face.

Megan carefully parked the car, got out and slipped on her waterproof jacket. Then she went into the office and picked up her helmet. It wasn't **her** helmet of course, but she was beginning to think of it in those terms, and she stroked it before she put it on her head, thinking this would be the last time she'd borrow it.

This afternoon was going to be full of last times.

'Hello?' The steadily falling snow muffled her voice as she went back outside, but the visibility wasn't too poor: the other side of the valley was still discernible, more or less, and she hoped this was as bad as it would get, although the snow was already starting to stick and she could see her footprints across the yard, which led her to worry how she was going to get home if it got any worse.

She heard a voice call from the direction of one of the barns, and as she realised who it was, her heart somersaulted and her breath caught in her throat.

'I didn't expect to see you,' she said, as she walked in out of the snow to find Nathan saddling the horses.

'Sorry,' he said. 'I know Petra was supposed to be taking you, but she's had to go out.'

Somehow Megan wasn't as surprised as she should have been. It seemed inevitable Nathan would be the one to go riding with her today. Fitting, almost. A kind of final goodbye.

Gosh, she was starting to get a bit morbid, so to shake the feeling she stepped forward with a smile and patted the satchel which she had slung diagonally over her shoulder and across her chest.

'I've got cake,' she said.

'And I've got a flask of hot chocolate.' He pointed to a small rucksack on top of a bale of hay. 'Don't worry,' he added, as he glanced out through the wide-open doors. 'The snow will stop in a minute.'

'It will? Are you some kind of weather guru?'

'Not exactly. Look at the sky.'

Megan glanced up, and sure enough, the occasional hint of blue could be seen between the clouds, and even as she watched the falling snowflakes became lighter.

'Quick,' Nathan said. 'Let's get out into it so that at least you can say you've ridden in the snow.'

'I don't quite think snow actually falling was what I meant.'

'I thought that was the whole point of these rides?'

'Yes, it was, but I think Jeremy got slightly the wrong end of the stick. He meant me to go riding when it was snowing, but I meant riding in the snow. There is a difference.'

'There is. Are you still happy to go out? It's only a couple of inches deep, maybe a little more on the hillside.'

'Let's go.' The decision was made, and there was no point in backing out of it now. She was here, the horses were ready, there was snow on the ground and still some falling. She didn't think she could go through this a second time, seeing Nathan's ruggedly handsome face and having to say goodbye to him all over again.

The horses didn't seem to mind being out in the weather one little bit. Their ears were pricked and Sherbet pranced slightly as if she was excited. Megan patted her neck and shushed her, and once again the mare fell into step behind Hercules, who arched his neck and lifted his tail, showing off slightly.

They made their way along the path above the fields, and when Megan looked back everything was blanketed in a thin layer of white; the scene was monochrome, in shades of grey, with her bright red car in the stables' car park being the only splash of colour for miles around.

Megan was soon lost in thought as she gazed at Nathan's back, gently swaying to the rhythm of the horse. Today was bittersweet; bitter because she was coming to the end of Jeremy's gifts and also because she wouldn't visit the stables again. But sweet because she was experiencing the last thing that Jeremy had organised for her, and also because she was on horseback and she was with a man she would dearly have loved to have gotten to know much, much better, if only she dared.

'Shit!' Nathan exclaimed. He pulled his horse to a sudden stop, and Sherbet almost walked into the back of Hercules.

The mare jerked, and Megan was jolted out of her reverie.

'What is it?' she asked.

'Look over there.' He pointed, and at first Megan couldn't see anything, and when she did, she wasn't quite sure of its significance.

'The fence has been cut,' Nathan explained.

'How can you tell?'

'Because I was in that field a couple of hours ago, and it was intact then. Not only that, but I also can't see any sign of Storm or Midnight.'

'Don't they belong to Charity and Luca?'

'That's right; they were in here with Mabel, that horse over there, and the two Shetlands. They are still here, but there's no sign of the others. Do you mind if we take a closer look?'

Megan could tell he was worried, even though he was trying to hide it. 'Of course not.'

'There's a gate further along. We don't use it often, but we should be able to get through it. If not, would you mind waiting here with the horses while I go on foot?'

'I don't mind at all,' she replied, but when they got to the gate, thankfully Nathan was able to open it with a bit of a struggle and a lot more cursing, and when he held it open for her, she led the two horses through before getting back on again. Nathan jumped into the saddle and took the lead once more.

The field was a large one, stretching from the path they were just on, right down to the road. It had fences along three sides and a dry stone wall running alongside the road which Megan knew carried on for a fair few miles. When they got closer to the fence even Megan could tell that it hadn't just collapsed – it had been cut. The wire had been peeled back to allow enough room for a horse to walk through, and there were hoofprints leading through it and across the neighbouring field.

But what was more worrying were the boot prints which accompanied the two sets of hooves.

'Rustlers,' Nathan muttered.

'Do you really think the horses have been stolen?' Megan asked incredulously.

'Pretty sure of it. Why else would you cut a fence and lead two horses out?' He turned to her and she could see the anger in his eyes and the hardness of his jaw. 'If you hadn't wanted to go for a ride in the snow, we wouldn't have noticed they were missing until this evening. Thank you.'

She was about to argue he had nothing to thank her for and it had been pure luck, when he swivelled in his saddle, his eyes scanning the road, and cried, 'There! See it?'

Megan saw a boxy dark blue vehicle parked on the road by the side of the wall. It was some distance away, and she had to squint to see it. 'Do you think it's the thieves?'

'It might be. Let's assume it is.' Nathan undid a couple of zips and thrust his hand into a pocket deep inside his jacket. Pulling out a mobile phone, he stabbed at it, put it to his ear, listened for a second, then swore. 'No signal.' Shaking his head, he put his phone away. 'I'm going to see what's what,' he said, 'but I'd like you to do me a favour, if you can. I can't get any signal to phone Petra or the police, so could you go back to the stables and ring them from there? Tell them we've had two horses stolen.'

'Do you think it's wise to go down there?' She narrowed her eyes at the barely visible horsebox on the road.

'I'm going to have to,' Nathan said. His face was grim.

'It might be dangerous,' she pointed out. If she thought pleading might work, she'd beg him not to go – she'd had enough worry over the years with Jeremy and his job, although she suspected she hadn't known the half of it, thank goodness. The last thing she wanted was to worry about Nathan.

Nathan nodded in acknowledgement. 'It might be, but I can't do nothing. Please go back to the stables, as fast as you can, but don't put yourself at any risk. I'll be back soon.'

There was nothing else for it. Megan knew that time was critical and she had to get in touch with the police as soon as possible, but she wasn't happy about leaving him on his own.

'Please take care,' she whispered. 'I'd hate it if anything happened to you.'

Nathan shot her a surprised look, and for one second she thought she'd gone too far and said something inappropriate. But then a smile lit up his face, and it was that which kept her warm as she turned her horse and headed back up the field.

Nathan watched her go, a frown creasing his forehead. Although it was only about half a mile back to the stables, he didn't like her going alone. But on the other hand, he couldn't simply sit on his horse and do nothing when there was a chance he might be able to stop the thieves. And he certainly couldn't allow her to go with him. What if that horsebox really did belong to the rustlers? He'd never forgive himself if he put her in harm's way.

Pushing his concern for Megan to the back of his mind, Nathan concentrated on what was happening down the road, and anger coursed through him.

How dare anyone come onto Petra's property and steal what wasn't theirs! If he caught them, he would...

He sighed. The chances of catching them were slim; it had been snowing for nearly two hours on and off, and although the tracks looked relatively fresh, he suspected the horses were long gone, and the vehicle in the layby down on the road was probably someone making a quick phone call.

Nevertheless, he followed the tracks straight across the field as the ground angled steadily downwards towards the layby and a gate set into the wall. It would probably only have taken the thieves minutes to park up, use bolt cutters on the gate, walk up the field and snip the fence, before catching the two horses and returning the way they'd come. It would have taken them half an hour, if that. God knows where those animals were now. They could be twenty miles away in any direction.

Gritting his teeth, his jaw aching from tension, Nathan drew closer, but as he did so he spied a horse's dark head above the top of the wall. The vehicle was definitely a horsebox: its back end was open and a ramp was down. Nathan could see two men at the front end of the horse trying to encourage it up the ramp, but the animal was having none of it. Midnight hated horseboxes and he would do anything in his power not to get into one. Luca's horse could be a bit of a handful at the best of times, but he could be an absolute nightmare to load, as the two men were finding out.

Nathan sat a little straighter in the saddle and craned his neck to peer into the back of the box. He could see a horse's rump in its gloomy depths. That must be Storm. They wouldn't have had any trouble with her at all and it was only because Midnight was refusing to get in it, that the thieves hadn't already driven off.

There was no time to lose. At any moment Midnight might give in and allow himself to be led onto the van and then they'd be away, and Nathan wouldn't have a hope in hell of catching them.

There **was** one thing he could do though – he could get the registration. The horsebox would probably be stolen, but it was better than nothing. It meant he'd have to get quite a bit closer though, so he led Hercules to a low-growing bush and slipped off his back, tying the reins firmly to the bare branches. The horse immediately pawed at the snow to reach the poor grazing underneath, lowered his head and began to nibble on the grass.

Nathan left him to it, and hunched over, scurrying down the field until he came to the wall. Using it as a shield, he crept along it, trying to get as close to the horsebox as he dared.

He could hear the two men cursing, and the gelding's annoyed squeals and snorts. The horse's hooves clattered on the tarmac, and the noise would hopefully cover any sound Nathan might make.

He was just about to stick his head over the wall and try to read the number plate, when a thought struck him...and his hand went to his pocket as a plan began to form.

With her heart in her mouth and fear for Nathan making her pulse soar, Megan headed back to the stables, all the while glancing over her shoulder to check on Nathan's progress. He was going to get hurt, she simply knew it, and the thought made her blood run cold.

She'd only trotted Sherbet for a few paces, when she tried phoning the stables. No signal.

A few more paces and still nothing.

'Come on,' she muttered, and Sherbet flicked her ears back. 'Not you, you're a good girl,' she told the horse, not wanting the mare to pick up on her nerves.

When Megan glanced back again, the field with its mutilated fence was out of sight, and so was Nathan, and her worry escalated to slightly short of panic.

Thank god, she finally had a signal.

She didn't bother with 999, though. Instead, she called a familiar number and prayed the man on the other end was available and close by.

'Fonzo, it's Megan. I need your help.'

'Whatever you need, you've got it.'

'Where are you?'

'Where do you want me to be?'

'On the road going east out of Picklewick, there's a blue van – I think it's a horsebox – pulled into a layby about three to four miles out of the village. I believe the occupants are attempting to steal two horses. A friend of mine has gone to try to stop them.'

'On my way. ETA five to seven minutes. Megan, are you okay? You're not in any danger?'

'I'm safe. I'm on the track above the road.'

'Good. Stay there. Jeremy would come back to haunt me if I let anything happen to you. Leave it to the police – I'll radio it in.'

'Thanks, Fonzo.' She heard him activate his car's siren and guessed it wouldn't be too long before Nathan heard it, too. 'And Fonz? Please make sure Nathan isn't hurt.'

'Nathan?'

'My friend.'

'Describe him.'

Megan did the best she could.

'Got it. You take care. I'll speak to you later.'

Fonzo ended the call, and Megan blew out her cheeks. She could rely on him utterly, the same way she could rely on any of Jeremy's former colleagues. Fonzo had partnered with Jeremy for several years before Jeremy had become ill, and she knew her husband's death had hit Fonzo hard. She'd never forget the tears running down his cheeks, or the words he'd said at Jeremy's funeral. The service had been memorable and moving, the police presence giving it added poignancy. Even now, almost two years on, all Megan needed to do was pick up the phone and someone would be there for her. And boy, was she glad of that now. If she'd gone through the emergency services' switchboard it would have taken longer for them to send a vehicle, and she had a feeling time wasn't on Nathan's side.

There was one more call Megan had to make before she turned Sherbet around and headed back to Nathan, and she got through to the stables on the first try.

To her surprise, Petra answered.

'I thought you were out,' Megan began, before swiftly adding, 'Never mind. I've got some bad news.' She told Petra exactly what she'd told the police, with the added information that they were on their way. 'One of them is, at least – he was my husband's partner, but he's called for backup. If that van is trying to steal your horses, there's a fair chance they'll be stopped before they get too far.'

Petra had been remarkably quiet as Megan relayed what had happened, but as soon as she stopped, Petra swore loudly.

'Where did you last see Nathan?' Petra demanded.

'Halfway down the field heading towards the layby.'

'I know it. I'm on my way. Where are you?'

'I'm on the track above the fields.'

'Okay, I'll tell Amos to expect you. He'll see to Sherbet. And Megan? **Thank you**.'

Petra ended the call abruptly and Megan guessed she was probably leaping into the Land Rover this very second. Although she'd heard the concern and fear in Petra's voice, she'd also heard a core of steel and determination underlying it, and she knew that in a crisis such as this, the woman wouldn't fall apart.

And neither would Megan, who had already turned around and was trotting back along the path, dread coursing through her. If anything should happen to Nathan, she'd never be able to forgive herself.

There were certain things Nathan always carried with him, his mobile phone being one of them, although that was next to useless at this very moment. Another thing was his multipurpose knife. It was rare he didn't find a use for it when he was out and about on the farm. He never took it to the village with him, but he was never without it when he was at work. And as he reached for it, he knew exactly what use he'd put it to today.

Stealthily he crept further along the wall until he was level with the cab. Risking a quick peep, he saw the men had their backs to him, trying to control Midnight who was practically sitting on his haunches and refusing to budge.

Taking a chance, in one fluid movement Nathan scaled the wall and dropped down silently onto the other side, the grassy verge and the snow cushioning any noise his boots might otherwise have made.

Crouching, he moved around to the front of the vehicle, out of sight of the men, then pulled his knife out of his pocket and opened it. It wasn't a very big knife and the blade wasn't very long, but it should hopefully serve the purpose.

Without hesitation, Nathan drew his arm back and plunged it with all his might into the driver's side wheel, the blade sinking up to its hilt in the rubber.

Crumbs, that had been easier than he'd anticipated, Nathan thought, before jerking the blade free, but as he did it made a loud popping hiss that could be heard even above the noise of the horse and the cursing of the two men.

Nathan flinched and stuck his head around the bumper, fearing the worst.

It was as he thought, the thieves had heard it, and they had both turned around.

He quickly snatched his head back, but he knew he'd been seen. One of them shouted, 'Oi!' and Nathan swallowed nervously. He could stick up for himself, but he was no superhero and he didn't fancy his chances against two of them. And neither did he want to risk a confrontation when he had a knife in his hand.

Leaping to his feet, he drew his arm back and threw the knife as far as he could into the field. Then he debated whether to run or fight. But as he dithered he heard a scraping noise. Damn it! One of them was holding a tyre iron in his hand and dragging it menacingly across the tarmac.

That decided it – he'd have to run. The pair of them might have twenty years on him, but he was fit and he knew the terrain like the back of his hand, and he hoped they wouldn't be bothered to chase him, but would be more interested in getting Midnight into the van and making their escape.

He dreaded to think what they'd do though, when they found out they couldn't. They might well decide to take their anger out on him, and as much as he loved the horses, he wasn't going to risk his life for them.

Nathan propelled himself forward and dived towards the wall, scrambling up and over it. But as he landed on the other side, his foot slipped from underneath him and he fell backwards. His head hit the stone wall with a sickening thud, and for a second lights exploded in his eyes and his vision blurred.

He lay there, winded and dazed, unable to focus.

Thanking god he was still wearing his hard hat, he vaguely wondered how much protection it would provide if the men decided to give him a good kicking and, feeling sick, he heard the clang of metal on stone and the scrabble of boots as one, or both of them attempted to scale the wall.

Bracing himself, all he could do was to lie there and await his fate, and hope it wouldn't be too bad.

'Rozzers!' one of the men shouted.

Nathan took a second to understand what had been said, and as he did so he heard sirens in the distance, and he closed his eyes and let out a breath.

'Thank you,' he whispered, his lips numb. Megan had probably got a signal a short distance along the track and he thanked god for her.

Trying to gather his wits, he heard the thud of boots on the road, the rattle of the ramp being lifted and the sound of a horse's hooves. He guessed they'd let Midnight go and were now trying to get away with Storm. The engine started and revved, and the horsebox lurched into motion.

They wouldn't get far, not with a punctured tyre.

Terrified Midnight would panic at the sound of the approaching sirens, Nathan dragged himself to his feet and slumped against the wall. He felt dizzy and his head ached, but at least he could now focus properly. And what he saw turned his heart to ice.

Midnight was careering down the road, his head high, his tail out like a streamer, and from his stiff movements Nathan could tell the horse was petrified.

There was only one thing for it.

Hauling himself up onto the wall, Nathan balanced precariously on its top.

Flashing blue lights in the distance signified the imminent arrival of the police, and he knew Midnight would whirl around and head back in his direction. The horse was wearing a halter and he also had a lead rope attached to it. Nathan's only chance of stopping the creature's headlong flight would be to throw himself at the lead rope and hope he caught hold of it. The horse might drag him, but his weight should slow the animal down enough to get him into the field.

As a plan, it stank, but Nathan couldn't see any other option.

He more or less fell off the wall as he tried to get down, and while he waited anxiously for Midnight to gallop back up the road, he prayed no one came past him going in the other direction, because they'd meet the horse head on and—

A crunch from behind made him cry out, and he lurched around.

The horsebox had come to a halt further up the road and was listing on the punctured side, the damaged wheel in a ditch. The two men tumbled out of the cab, staggered, then ran, as a horse's squealing neigh rang out.

Nathan felt sick – Storm was trapped in the box, possibly injured and certainly terrified, and he hesitated, torn between wanting to help her and needing to catch Midnight.

Hooves galloping up the road had him spinning back to face Midnight's direction again. Steeling himself for what was about to happen, his head pounded and his pulse raced, and he swallowed convulsively.

The animal came into view—

And Nathan sagged with relief. Petra was astride Midnight, hunched low over the horse's back as the beast raced down the centre of the road; but it was a controlled gallop and not the frantic headlong flight Nathan had been expecting.

Instinctively he dashed to the gate, swung it open and stood back. With a yell, Petra leant to the side, guiding the panicked creature towards it, and the pair of them plunged through the opening and charged up the slope. Nathan caught a glimpse of wide nostrils and flattened ears, and saw Petra's triumphant expression.

One down, one to go, he thought wildly, as he pulled the gate shut and stumbled up the road towards the horsebox.

Storm was still neighing, her calls sending shivers of fear through him, and when he reached the back of the horsebox and fumbled with the fastenings with numb, unresponsive fingers, he dreaded what he might find.

'It's okay, my sweet, it's okay, I'm here, we'll soon get you out,' he crooned, forcing himself to remain calm, knowing she would sense his fear if he didn't. Taking a deep, steadying breath, he undid the back and opened the door, then dropped the ramp down slowly.

Sirens were loud behind him, blue flashing lights illuminating the interior of the box, and he didn't want to look, but he knew he had to...

Storm was balancing awkwardly, trying to compensate for the tilt of the floor under her hooves as the vehicle canted over, but apart from the fear in her eyes and the flaring of her nostrils, she seemed unharmed, and he let his breath out in a whoosh.

Startled, Storm jerked her head, and Nathan hastily resumed speaking to her in a soothing, calm tone until she relaxed enough for him to approach without the risk of him getting hurt.

'There's a good girl,' he murmured. 'Who's a good girl. We'll soon get you out of this nasty horsebox.'

Slowly and gently, careful not to alarm her any more than she was already, he inched forward until he was able to untie the rope, then he backed her up until she felt the slope of the ramp under her hooves, and he guided her down it.

As Nathan tied her to the outside of the box, relief and spent adrenalin made him feel sick and giddy, and he leant against the side of the vehicle, his heart labouring and his head spinning, before he leisurely slipped to the ground.

The last thing he saw was Megan's tear-stained face, and the last thing he heard was her crying, 'Don't die, Nathan. I love you. Please don't die.'

CHAPTER NINE

'You're a bloody idiot, that's what you are,' Amos said. 'Tell him, Petra, tell him what an idiot he is.'

'I don't need to – I think you've told him enough times,' Petra replied.

She gave Nathan one of her looks, but he didn't take offence. He knew they were right, he had been an idiot; but, damn it, people shouldn't be allowed to get away with taking things that didn't belong to them. Especially animals. They had feelings and people who loved them. It wasn't like nicking a quad bike (although that was bad enough), or stealing a telly.

'I give up,' Amos said, throwing his hands in the air. 'Perhaps you can make him see sense.' This last was aimed at Megan.

Nathan winced as he turned his head. Megan was sitting on the sofa in Petra's living room. She was worrying at her lips with her teeth, and they looked red and very kissable. He couldn't take his eyes off her mouth.

'You might have died,' she repeated. She'd mentioned this at least twenty times over the course of the past five hours. An ambulance had shown up at some point whilst he was lying in the lane and had taken him to the hospital to be checked out, and Megan had refused to leave his side.

'But I didn't,' he replied for the twentieth time. 'I'm still here.' His tone was gentle – he understood what this was costing her. That she'd come back for him meant the world to him. It had also worried him senseless when he'd realised she hadn't obeyed his instruction to return to the stables. His own safety meant nothing compared to hers.

He vaguely remembered some copper giving her short shrift too, but it was only when he was waiting to be seen by a doctor that he'd discovered Jeremy had been a policeman, and the main reason the "rozzers" had shown up so fast was because Megan had phoned one of them directly, and hadn't dialled 999.

'They should have kept you in for observation,' Amos grumbled. 'In my day, they would have.'

'It's still your day,' Harry said.

Everyone was gathered in the living room of the stables, along with the two dogs, the cat, and Fred, the cockerel, who had managed to sneak in amidst all the fuss. So much for being advised to get some rest, Nathan thought, although rest was the last thing on his mind. He was exhausted and his head hurt something rotten, but he was also high on adrenalin. Not from the attempted theft, but from what Megan had said to him as he lay on the tarmac, feeling less than splendid.

He'd tried to speak to her about it when they were waiting at the hospital for him to be checked over, but she'd refused to discuss it, and for a while he'd wondered if he'd imagined it. But surely not, because the first thing he'd said when he'd come round was 'I love you, too,' and she'd smiled so widely it was as though the sun had come out.

A huge yawn escaped him and he briefly closed his eyes.

Maybe he was tired, after all.

'Come on, everyone out,' Petra ordered. She was looking knackered, too. It had been a rough day all round. But at least the thieves had been arrested, the horses were in their stalls, neither of them the worse for their ordeal, and the only injury was his mild concussion. His helmet had saved him from what could have been a fractured skull if he hadn't been wearing it, and since he'd returned to the stables he'd been fussed over and coddled, and treated like a hero, much to his chagrin and embarrassment.

'Someone should stay with him,' Amos advised, looking pointedly at Megan.

'It's late, I should be getting home,' she said.

'Stay here for the night,' Petra suggested. 'It's dark and icy, and driving in those conditions should be avoided. We've got a couple of spare rooms.'

'I'd also better be going.' Nathan struggled to sit up, but Megan, who was nearest to him, having not moved further from him than a hair's breadth, pushed him back down.

'Not on your nelly. Petra, tell him. He can't go home like this.'

'Megan is right. You should both stay the night.'

Amos beamed. 'I've got a nice pot of hearty stew on the stove and some fresh bread to go with it. We'll have a bite to eat later, but it won't be ready for an hour, so let's leave Nathan in peace for a bit.'

'Megan, will you stay with him?' Petra asked, and Nathan narrowed his eyes at her. The sly cat was up to something and he had a pretty good idea what it was.

'Only if Nathan wants me to,' Megan said, darting a glance at him.

'I want you to,' he confirmed. They needed to have a chat about what they'd said to each other. Words such as those couldn't be unspoken, but he wanted to check it wasn't the heat of the moment that had been responsible for them.

He hoped to god that wasn't the case. Because, to his immense surprise, he found he meant what he'd said when he'd told her he loved her. Nathan couldn't believe he felt this way when he'd only known her for such a short time. Was that possible, or was his head injury more severe than the doctor had thought?

The room cleared, leaving him and Megan alone except for Patch, who had curled up at his master's feet and refused to move. Bemused, Nathan waited for the door to snick shut, then he turned his gaze on her. 'You said you love me. Is that true?'

'Do you honestly want to do this right now?'

He nodded, then wished he hadn't.

'Is the headache really bad?' she asked, seeing his pained face. 'I can get you some—' She made to rise, but he grabbed hold of her hand and pulled her back down. He felt as weak as a kitten, so he was grateful she sank into her chair without a fight.

'I'm fine,' he said. 'It's nothing I can't handle. Will you answer my question?'

She looked like a rabbit faced with a fox, all wide-eyed frozen terror. 'Do I have to?'

'I love you.'

'So you said.'

'I mean it.'

'We've only known each other for a couple of months.'

'We've known each other forever.'

'Jeremy...' She shrugged helplessly. 'I still love him.'

'Of course you do. I wouldn't expect anything else.'

'You don't mind?'

'Why would I?' Nathan shuffled in his seat, the cushions sucking him down. 'He's part of you.'

'But—'

'There is no but, not unless you want there to be.' He had to convince her. She was right in that they'd not known each other long, and they both had their issues – her husband, his reluctance to share his life with anyone – but the thought of not seeing her again made his very soul ache. She'd changed him, without meaning to, and without him realising, but there was no going back to the way he'd been before he'd met her. He didn't think she could go back, either. When he'd first set eyes on her she'd been in a dark place, but now light was shining out of her, and she was beginning to come to life again.

He so desperately wanted it to be with him.

'Okay, I admit it. It's true – I do love you.' She said it defiantly.

'Good, I'm glad.'

'Where do we go from here?' More defiance, as though she was daring him to come up with a plan that she could pick apart.

'I've no idea. Shall we take it one day at a time?'

She shrugged. Her head was lowered so he couldn't see her face. 'I suppose.' Then she peeped at him from underneath her lashes.

It was such a flirtatious and provocative thing for her to do that his breath hitched.

'How's the head?' she asked again.

'What head?'

'The one on your shoulders, that nearly got knocked off.'

'Can't feel a thing,' he replied, cheerfully. It was true, he felt no pain, only a burgeoning elation and a quiet joy.

'In that case, kiss me,' she commanded.

For once in his life, Nathan was happy to do as he was told.

And when his lips met hers, he knew he would be happy to kiss her for the rest of his life.

'Are you sure you're okay?' Megan shot Nathan a worried look. It was far too soon for him to be on the back of a horse, but he'd insisted on riding today. Apparently, he "owed" her a ride to compensate for the one that ended so abruptly and so dramatically less than a week ago.

'I'm fine, stop fussing.'

'I like fussing. And you secretly like to be fussed over,' she replied, inching Sherbet closer to Hercules so she could nudge Nathan with her knee.

'Do not,' he retorted, but his broad grin gave him away.

They'd seen each other every day since the horse-rustling incident, and Megan couldn't get enough of him.

She still felt disloyal to Jeremy and she had an inkling the feeling might never entirely go away, but she also felt she had her husband's blessing, and she wondered if her falling in love again had been the sole purpose behind all those gifts. Although, to be fair, she still couldn't see how planting a wildflower garden at the back of their house was going to move that forward. It had been a solitary experience, except for her frequent visits to the garden centre and her chats with the middle-aged couple who ran it.

Nevertheless, she embraced her newfound happiness and was determined never to make Nathan feel second best. Because he wasn't. Nathan was lovely, kind, thoughtful, and sexy, and she vowed to try to make him happy every single day; he deserved nothing less. They both deserved a second chance at love, and although theirs was new and fresh, it didn't mean there was no depth to it.

And who'd have guessed that the surly, reticent man she'd met in December would turn out to be such a romantic? As this ride across the hills on a blimmin' freezing but very bright day in January testified.

Snow lay thickly on the ground, drifting to a couple of feet deep in places, and the horses' breath steamed around their heads as they plodded gamely up the blanketed path. The air was calm and incredibly still, and Megan could see for miles. The only sound was the crunch of snow underfoot, the jingle of the tack, and the occasional bleat of a sheep from the fields far below.

When they came to the ruined farmhouse, Nathan tied the horses to a scrubby tree growing through the middle of it, and he brushed the snow off the remains of one of the walls and spread a blanket over it for her to sit on.

With a cup of hot chocolate in one hand and a slice of her latest creation in the other (red velvet cake with a Valentine heart decoration on the top), Megan's soul was filled with peace and her heart brimmed with happiness. And when they'd finished their drinks and Nathan gathered her in his arms, she was warmed from the inside out by his love.

He was her future, and she felt so incredibly excited to embrace all that life had to offer.

Magical, that's what their love was...**magical**.

The Stables on Muddypuddle Lane Series

Spring

Summer

Autumn

Winter

Valentine Kisses

The Patter of Tiny Feet

Wedding Bells

Christmas

About Etti

Etti Summers is the author of wonderfully romantic fiction with happy ever afters guaranteed.

She is also a wife, a mum, a pink gin enthusiast, a veggie grower and a keen reader.